ACCOUNTANT ON THE EDGE

ACCOUNTANT ON THE EDGE

Arthur C. DeLozier

ISBN-13: 9780985706746
ISBN-10: 0985706740
ISBN-10: 0-9857067-5-9 (ebook)
ISBN-13: 978-0-9857067-5-3 (ebook)
Library of Congress Control Number: 2016913345
A.C. DeLozier, Maryville, TN

To my profession. I was never bored.
To my clients and friends. You supplied great material.
To my family. Without your support this work would not be possible.

CHAPTER 1

MORNING

I see our office door ease open. Lieutenant Allison Bryce slowly enters the room, pushing the door wide with her hip and rolling sideways, being careful with the tall cups she holds high. *Looks like Starbucks coffee from here*, I think. And she's followed my advice: take two cups and use the second one for insulation, along with the cardboard band. But she appears to be feeling the heat in her hands anyway; her lips are tight lines of concentration.

Bypassing her own desk, she edges to the front of mine and stops. She cautiously lowers both cups to my desktop and steps back to blow on her fingertips. Then, looking up to my eyes, she nods her greeting. I lean back and silently greet her in return: a brief hand wave with my arms still folded across my increasingly ample middle. She smiles at the gesture; it's familiar to her, I suppose. Or maybe that's only relief I'm seeing in her face—relief at having just completed an annual travail: she's come back to work after two weeks of leisure, and she's brought me my coffee … and both on the same day. I huff through my nose at that thought—not that it's especially hard coming back from vacation but that she's bringing me coffee at my desk. See, I'd once made the mistake of telling her to get me a cup of coffee. 'Nuff said?

But, you know, I can imagine it being tough having to return to the grind after being away for weeks on a luxury vacation, too. Maybe that's why I never take them. And she's likely remembered on her drive in this morning that she'd promised to bring something back for me—something nice. "Something you'll really appreciate," she'd said. So she's bringing me coffee from the Starbucks beside the station. She's stopped on the way in—just like last year and the years before that. *Nice.* I reach for the coffee and manage a long, appreciative smile—she's actually easy to smile at—and I see she's ... different. Somehow she really looks ... healthier? I'll have to tell her that. *Later.* In fact, if I'm not mistaken, she's also shortened her hair a bit, and she's bought herself a new outfit, one with a very short skirt. So maybe that's to go with the hair?

Seconds tick by with us examining each other and grinning stupidly. I think she's waiting on me to speak first while I'm waiting for her to talk, to maybe ask about what all I've been doing. And I guess I am—waiting, that is. See, despite what Allison says, I'm not an overly talkative fellow—I'm not. I'm just, well—I'm the kind of person who thinks best when I'm talking. Like I say to her, the understanding of a story is in the retelling of it. She says I'm exhausting. Regardless, I guess I've missed her—but she's got to end her own vacation. After all, she's the one who wanted the time away.

"OK, Detective Eltie," she says—finally—tossing her dark hair to one side. "Let's have it. You look like you're bursting at the seams to tell me all about that," she says, nodding at the enlarged photograph centered on my desk pad where I'd been studying it, "besides looking like you've spent the entire night here. And now you're gonna make me ask about what you're working on before you'll say, aren't you? So are you tired or just feeling ornery and sorry for yourself?"

I consider my response—*maybe all of the above?*—as I straighten in my chair, rubbing my face and pushing my sixty-two-year-old wrinkles to my ears. It feels so good. If I had more hair, I'd be running my fingers through it, too; I remember that as having felt kinda satisfying.

"So, Cole, what's with the gun?" she asks, not waiting for my reply, or else expecting only a smart-ass answer. She turns the photo. "The nine-millimeter Beretta." The lady knows her weapons, too.

"Yeah ... yeah," I confirm. "But, you know, Detective Bryce, somehow, each year, you manage to pick the absolute worst time to schedule vacations. It's amazing. And it's been a ..." I pause. *Won't matter.* Allison seldom feels inclined to accept guilt without resistance—especially if it's being applied by me. And, like she said, I probably am feeling frustrated and sorry for myself. *Just irrelevant verbiage*—like she also says. "It's just been a hard couple of weeks," I finish. "And now this one here." I tap the picture.

"Tell me," she says, raising her coffee cup, sipping, and setting it back on the desktop, well away from the photo. "But first. ..." She turns and pulls her chair around so she's mostly facing me when she sits. "OK. Start at the beginning." She leans forward, resting on one elbow, her fingers bracketing her chin.

Complete attention. I take a deep breath and adjust myself on my seat cushion. My butt hurts at the base of my spine, probably from sitting in one place too long. "Weirdest thing, Bryce," I begin. "Did you hear anything on the news about the accountant—the CPA—who'd been blasted away on his own doorstep? You did? Well, it's about him ... the accountant. And not because of his being an accountant, you know, but, like, from being a writer!"

Her eyes narrow. As I might have mentioned, Allison likes her stories straight, with little coloring and few tangents. And I'm the storyteller. Hard to believe we make such a good team.

"See, we—I was called to this guy's house down near Gulfport, down near the water. Shots had been fired. An old woman living a few houses away heard gunshots and called it in. It's a rough neighborhood there, but, you know, it's nowhere near as rough as it used to be, back when you were apt to hear shots several times a week. Remember?" Allison probably doesn't; I've got about thirteen or fourteen years on her—both in age and in seniority.

A single nod.

"Well, when I pull up, a couple of patrol cars are there already, and an ambulance is turning the corner. Seems a man's down, lying there on the walkway leading to the house, the accountant's house. Dead already according to the patrolman. Face blasted off, ear to ear, hair to chin. Grisly. Gate to the yard—open—no pets noted." That last part wasn't in my notes; I just remember it. "And glass from maybe a car window was scattered on the pavement out front. But, see, I don't know if the broken glass had anything to do with the dead guy; it could have already been there. Maybe no relationship."

Another quick nod; Allison's encouraging me forward.

"Anyway, somebody had already called the ambulance, and about the time they had the guy loaded up, the guy's daughter comes pulling in. She immediately recognizes him by his clothing—sneakers and shirt—and goes to pieces." I push up my notepad from my breast pocket and flip through its pages. "Andrea James—that's the daughter's name. His name was Maxwell Anderson." I lay the pad on top my desk—open for easy reference.

"While James is getting herself together, I look around the house and find a shotgun, a Mossberg twenty gauge, in the back corner of the hallway. I smell it. Smells freshly fired but who knows—it's a shotgun." Allison knows how residue odors linger in hunting rifles and shotguns. "I immediately think someone living there could've offed the old man—domestic stuff, you know—but the daughter says her father lived alone and she'd been with friends, out shopping since the morning. She and the friends had lunch together, she says, and she was bringing a sandwich for Dad, since it'd been a while since she'd seen him. With her saying that, I considered it might've been a suicide—you know, lonely father and such?—but, with a head wound like that, the old guy couldn't have taken two steps out the door." I thumb to the next page in my notepad.

"Forensics collected the shotgun. Birdshot loads in it. Two shells in the clip—bolt action. One shell in the chamber—spent. Smudge on the stock that could've been blood.

"When they'd finished up with the scene, I went back outside to look around. Saw just normal stuff for old folks living in Gulfport: lots of plants in the yard, allamandas, fruit trees in the back, birdbaths, a few bird feeders hanging about—remains of a really big one hanging from a chain in the backyard—probably rotted and fallen down, I think at the time. Then I see what looks like blood droplets on the pavers leading to the garage ... and the garage is empty like maybe someone's taken the old guy's car." I refer to the page again. "Oh yeah. Spent shotgun shell on the pavers. ... Forensics found the shell on the ground."

I glance at Allison. She's still listening.

"I follow the drops back toward the house and notice pellet holes in the wood and framing at the side of the back window—the old guy's bedroom window. And the window's not broken or recently replaced, but the wood around it is pretty-well chewed up; pellets were birdshot." I see the question flicker in Allison's eyes. "Forensics was still there," I explain. "See, I got them to check out the pellet holes, and they dug some out to take back. What's the matter? You think I wouldn't know birdshot when I see it?"

She rolls her eyes.

"Anyway, while Forensics is still there, I note the blood sprinkles and ask for a sample comparison with Mr. Anderson's blood—heaven knows there's enough of it out front, puddled on the sidewalk. Then—listen to this—I see more blood in the grass besides what's on the pavers, so I begin to think the assailant might've injured himself in the attack ... and dripped blood as he came around the house ... to steal the car." I pause, unsmiling, sage, allowing the import of my discernment to settle. "You know, that blood sample might very well lead us to the killer," I add, uncertain of her level of discernment.

"Go on," she says.

I sigh. "Meantime, the daughter, James, gets herself under control and asks if we could talk later on—maybe in the afternoon. Says she'd be better able to talk then. So I leave to swing by the restaurant she'd mentioned—cashier remembered them—and by the morgue to see if the medical examiner had made a start. They had. Main thing: Forensics found JW tracts—Jehovah's Witnesses' tracts—and a *Watchtower* magazine on the old guy, or under him anyway … and several more of both publications stacked just inside the gate—like they were being stashed for the minute. Made me wonder."

Allison presses forward, waiting for me to explain this thought.

"See, Bryce, the medical examiner shared some early info with me: initial body-examine stuff, clothing inventory. And, you know, that was what I thought was kinda strange: except for the JW stuff, the old man's pockets were empty. Nothing. Nada."

She wrinkles her brow. "If he'd just stepped out of the house for a minute," she counters, "he wouldn't have had anything in his pockets anyway, would he? Except for maybe a house key."

I shake my head. "No, probably not. I didn't think to ask if they'd found the house unlocked either. The door was open when I got there—but that might not matter anyway, now that I think about it …" Allison's eyes tighten. She says nothing, but I realize I'm going in another direction now—doing my think-aloud routine.

"So I go back toward Gulfport, to the house, and only one cop's still there. He's waiting on me because Forensics has finished and the daughter's asked after me. We sit in the kitchen at the table. Cookies and hot tea."

Allison sighs.

I continue, "I want to ask about the old man's JW activities in the neighborhood, thinking that maybe he's pissed somebody off. You know? Got into an argument or something and things got heated? Anyway, the daughter gives me a weird look … like you just did, Bryce." I grin because she's not certain whether I'm joking—and I am.

I go on, "The daughter, Andrea James, looks rather blank when I ask. She tells me her father's a Baptist and wasn't likely to be out proselytizing the neighborhood and discussing religion. She said he wasn't a 'works' guy and was rather private with his faith. She said he wouldn't have been out visiting and witnessing to the neighborhood in general. That just wasn't him.

"Then she says she wants to tell me something else: See, she'd gone out back and seen her father's sneakers outside—on the back porch, on the steps—and that told her maybe it wasn't *his* ratty ol' tennis shoes she'd noticed back when they were carting the old man away. She says the newspaper guys have come and gone and that all reports have been made and that maybe the funeral home should've been called and so on ... but now she's thinking and bothered by the fact that she hadn't been able to look him over more carefully. 'That just maybe ...' she says.

"So I tell her that anything's possible. See? She looked so hopeful and stuff. Anyway, I didn't want to cause more hurt, you know?" Bryce nods her understanding. "So I tell her the lab has gone through his pockets and that absolutely nothing—other than the pamphlet—was found in his pockets. And I tell her the lab would give us more information about birthmarks and such later on. There's always hope, I say. Besides, I know she still has to go downtown to identify her father on the slab; she'll get her second look then.

"About that time, I ask her this question: 'Ms. James, was there someone you know of who may have wanted to do your father harm?' I was asking if there was someone she suspected of being capable of ... killing him. Maybe someone he'd worked with? A person who—"

Allison chuckles—surprising me—and immediately offers a half-assed apology for it. "Sorry," she says, "but the old guy was an accountant, wasn't he, Cole? I mean, just how dangerous can that occupation be? Maybe sharpened-pencil hazards, huh?" She remembers something else and puffs another giggle. "You know," she says, "I once dated a CPA—probably the most boring time in my life. Everything was so-so and structured. Safe and orderly. I bet this victim wouldn't have dared to cross even a ..." Her voice fades as she searches for a suitable example.

I chuckle, too, to break the long pause; she's made her point: accountants seldom, if ever, encounter violent conflict within their profession—unless they're caught with their hand in the till, I guess. Allison's probably thinking this murder's the result of a home invasion, a robbery that went wrong, or something else—something more probable—like I do. But that makes me think of something else: an old joke. "Imagine two accountants talking," I say. "Which accountant is the extrovert?"

Allison squints at me and barely shakes her head.

"He's the one looking at the other fellow's shoes!" I snort, laughing and slapping my thigh.

Silence.

"See?" I explain. "You made a—you reminded me of that joke. So I thought—"

"So what did Ms. Andrea James have to say?" she interrupts, encouraging me forward again. She wants to get back to the murder business.

"Hey, I've been saving that joke—"

"For a long, long time, I bet," she scoffs. "And James replied? ..."

Allison's eyeballing me over the tops of her glasses, waiting on me. I notice she's got rather nice eyes—good makeup. You know, maybe I should try to work out more often. Maybe not weightlifting again—the ol' back won't stand for that. But maybe yoga. *Yeah.*

"Ahem." She's still waiting.

"Well, for your information, Detective Bryce," I say, emphasizing her name, "Ms. James said her father actually *did* have a strong personality and that he had, in the past, been in several ticklish situations. Allow me to relate." I slide my top drawer out; a thick folder's lying there, crammed with loose photocopies and such. I ease it out and dramatically plop it on my desktop beside my notepad and flip open its top cover.

Allison sniffs again. "So you're about to tell me the old guy and an IRS agent mixed it up, inflicting serious paper cuts on several phalanges?" She's on a roll.

"Close," I say, maintaining my sagacious demeanor. "Her father *does* have a record on file, you know."

"What?"

I have her interest again. "Yeah. It seems that, around Christmastime, he almost got into it ... with a trucker, a tow-truck driver." I fish the one-page report from the pile.

"Assault and battery?"

"Close. You know how some malls with limited parking will contract with towing companies to boot certain cars, those with drivers who don't shop exclusively in the mall's stores? Yeah? Well, it seems Mr. Anderson had stepped next door to a pharmacy after having first dined at a restaurant in the strip mall. When he returned, he found a wheel lock fastened to the front tire of his car. Made him furious, it seems."

"Yeah? What happened?"

"Well, after retrieving his socket set and extension from out of his trunk, the old man proceeded to remove the boot. The tow-truck driver—six two maybe, beefy sort—thereafter joined the scene, about the same time as the old man was finishing up; he then threatened to beat him to a bloody pulp. It was just lucky a patrol car passed by about that time and noticed the gathering crowd."

"Well, whoopee. Saved the old man, did they? Was he injured?"

"Not exactly. Seems Mr. Anderson also packed a tire iron in his trunk and was using it when the officers intervened. He was trying to get at the driver who had, by then, fled to the cab of his tow truck. I'm not sure how much damage the old man might've inflicted on the big dude, but it could've been substantial." I inch my finger down the page. "The damage to the truck's door was quite impressive, according to this report."

Allison puffs her cheeks. "Capable of murder?" she asks, her voice low and slightly subdued. "I mean, the driver?"

"Dunno. When I checked the traffic files, I saw this entered report—but nothing had been done. The tow-truck driver apparently hadn't wished to pursue action … against a sixty-something-year-old fellow—unless it could be done without public notice. The officer states he'd allowed both parties to leave the premises with only warnings."

"So do you think the big dude had second thoughts and later decided to pay Mr. Anderson a visit at his home? With maybe a

gun? I know you boys have these big ol' egos you gotta protect."
Allison's eyes glitter; she's had a great vacation.

"Well, ma'am," I say, "I think an elevation of the parking-lot altercation is entirely possible ... but that might now be of a lesser priority for our investigatory attention. See, the daughter, Andrea, was initially somewhat vague when I asked her if she knew of someone who would want to harm her father. I expected her to laugh, just like you did, and to say that her dad *was* an accountant and so on, like you did. But she didn't. In fact, she said there might be quite a few people who would wish him harm."

"What?"

"Yeah. She said her father was writing a book and he'd kept notes ... and sometimes created stories using these notes." I pat the thick folder.

"What?" Allison is totally confused. "Let me see that file."

I turn it around and push it over to her. She riffles through the stapled packets, stopping to silently read headings. I continue, "Andrea said her father would often make up bedtime stories for her when she was a little girl, a child. And sometimes he'd pull out this folder where he'd kept notes—for inspiration, I suppose. Like I said, he was planning on writing a book someday when he retired. So, back then, he was apparently trying out some of his chapters on the kid, maybe seeing if there was interest in his yarns. Or maybe he was editing as he read."

"Was there?" Allison asks. "Interest, I mean?" She didn't look up from the stack of papers. "These appear to me to be copies of mostly typed pages—like for his book—but this top page in this group looks and reads like a threat letter."

"It is; they are—and were. There's more. According to the daughter, the old man received quite a few of these threat letters over the years ... and kept them. And then later used them in writing the chapters attached to some of these. See there." I point to the typed pages. "Maybe like a memory aid or something."

"Do you think the stories are true?"

"At first I didn't think so. The daughter said her father had recently received a big write-up in the *Times* about his book—the original proofs are apparently in his publisher's hands—and the article said the work was fiction. She said she'd never gone through the folder before—not until yesterday. Then she'd remembered the papers and went into her father's study to—"

"Forensics didn't get the folder?"

"No, not until I gave it to them to check for fingerprints and such. These here are all photocopied pages. Remember, they were still working with the outside crime scene at the time. She—the daughter, Andrea—gave me the file when I returned. She said then that his book was to be published as a fiction-type novel, and, well, she'd not seen the threatening notes until then—later in the afternoon. She said she'd remembered his stories to be rather boring when he was reading from this folder—full of accounting terms and situations—something really boring for a child."

"What'd the *Times* article say about the book?"

I point to one of the pages, an original. "I got that yesterday from the newspaper; it's a copy of the published article. It gives some info about Mr. Anderson, discusses the proposed release date, and summarizes some details of those chapters there and beneath that packet. And it hints at important names in the book." I nod meaningfully; the article promises a lot.

Allison is taking her time reading through the file. "So let me get this straight—"

"Why don't you just read one or two of those things, Allison, while I go get some breakfast? I have … and I've actually found them quite interesting. Not like high drama or anything but insightful in an understated sort of way. And not as lurid an exposé as promised in the *Times* article—I think that must have actually been an advertisement. Just read a few chapters yourself."

She sighs heavily, exhaling through her nose, and moves some stapled-together pages from the pile onto the open desktop. The photocopied cover page and the adhesive tape holding it in place on the stationery are both yellowed with age, but I can read the faded date at the top: June 1975.

"Good one," I say. "That's one of the earliest, but it's not one of the shorter chapters."

Allison glares up at me—she's obviously trying to humor me and wants me to know it. "So did he change the names in the book to protect the innocent?" she asks.

I ignore the sarcasm. "Gosh, I don't know for sure. Not entirely, I'd say. He used his own name in that one, and some of the people's names were in our records—they have police records. And the threat letters were definitely sent to him. But, you know, if you mean whether he changed any names, well, I suppose ..."

I'm looking at the top of Allison's head now; I don't believe she's still listening to me.

"Want me to leave you alone?" I ask.

She barely dips her noggin as she flips to the next page.

Guess so.

CHAPTER 2

JUNE 1975

"Hey, Max. Got a minute?"

Maxwell Anderson, graduate accountant and newest employee of Randal Minz, CPA, PA, slowly, reluctantly, emerged from his thought fog, blinking his eyes as he searched around for the source of this interruption.

The voice came again: "Here! Door!"

He looked up and over. *Oh yeah—there.* It was his boss, Randal, standing outside the doorway and leaning into the room, peering down on him from over the cardboard boxes stacked high alongside his desk.

"Oh … hey, Randal," he languidly replied, rolling his chair backward and away from his desk while thumbing his glasses to the bridge of his nose. His mind continued to resist this change of attention, wanting to continue on with its calculation of depreciation for those newly added assets on Mr. Jason W. Wilson's Form 1040 Schedule C. Max had actually never met the flesh-and-blood Mr. Jason W. Wilson, but, at this moment, he was intimately involved with this most important event in the man's life—or at least in the life of his part-time lawn-care business. *Sure.*

Still mentally shaking himself free, Max coughed and greeted again, "Hey, Randal. Whatcha need?" He'd been hired a few months earlier, straight out of college—or rather, while he was still in college and standing in the office of his favorite professor, Gene

McVeigh. He'd been summoned earlier that day, during his 10:00 a.m. Advanced Accounting and Interpretive Problems of Accounting for Business Combinations class, via a note dropped by his instructor onto the open page of his textbook: "Mr. Anderson," he'd then whispered to himself, deciphering the words of the familiar microscopic scrawl, "Have you the time to drop by my place—3:00 p.m. today—concerning employment? G.M." Max had arrived for the appointment about an hour early, and the rest was history: he'd been hired—the only student from among twenty-five classmates graduating from USF's Saint Pete campus in the spring of 1975 to have a job prior to graduation. This year, 1975, the final official year of the '70s recession and the year the Vietnam War ended, had begun like the decade's earlier years: with disaster for businesses and job seekers. Employment openings in the Tampa Bay area were few in number and very low paying, particularly in the accounting career field. The annual compensation amount then quoted to him was $7,900 ... and he'd jumped on it. Anyone in his graduating class of Spring 1975 would've taken it.

"So when are you guys going to clean up these boxes?" Randal asked, lightly patting the tall stack as he forced his way into the cramped room. "It's a fire hazard, you know—all these boxes in the doorway."

Max leaned back and rotated himself in place, his worn chair squealing like a pack of lonesome chihuahuas, to visually consult with his two office mates working at their respective desks, each man also facing a windowless wall and each wall also piled high with boxes stacked alongside desks. To his right, Gordon Moore, a heavyset young fellow about his age, conscientiously ignored him, continuing to furiously tap away at his calculator, adding up the long rows of numbers from the columnar pad on his desk. The second accountant, a much older white-haired fellow seated at the desk behind, simply glanced back at him and slowly affected an exaggerated shoulder shrug, his palms to the ceiling. *What? No opinion, Lou? Or maybe just not your problem?* Max would sure miss the old guy.

Lou—Louis no-middle-initial—Goldman had actually once owned this accounting practice, sharing office space and then selling out to Randal some seven or eight years prior, he'd said. He now only worked part-time for a few months each year, assisting with the income-tax preparations "just to keep my hand in." And as it was, his tour for this year was rapidly nearing its end ... and the boxes could stay where they were ... until next year.

Max rotated back to the door, to Randal. "What boxes?" he replied, his eyes wide and innocent.

"Smart-ass," Randal snarled, shaking his head but still smiling. His joke had fallen flat; he'd known very well that the file cabinets in the few other offices were filled to capacity and that the only other place to deposit the boxed records was in the hallway—and the hallway accumulation, stacked six rows high, was already an immediate threat to passersby. "Yeah, yeah, I know," he continued, pausing for dramatic effect. "We're totally out of space now, but remember ... we'll be moving soon ... to the new building." Ta-da! Randal had recently purchased an old house farther down Central Avenue and was renovating it for office space. "We'll have an entire file room there, guys! With space just for file cabinets and shelves." He rapped a box with his knuckles as he looked to each man, his gaze lingering, perhaps awaiting an upturned face or a question—but no questions came. The "guys" simply sat and nodded ... and waited, relatively certain the boss had not edged his way from his office in the front, down the long corridor, merely to harass them about their stacks or to talk about the new building; he had an intercom for that. They expected he'd next ask (order) them to work late tonight—again.

"So, Max," he said, breaking the extended silence, "would you like to go with me to look at the new place right now?" Still no response. "The carpenters are there, and I had planned on taking you out to VisualOptics anyway—to meet John and Howard. Oh, by the way, you're to start work there on Monday ... on the audit."

That was an announcement! What? Me? Audit? Max glanced sideways, over to Lou and Gordon. The old man bobbed his white-fringed head in return, approving and grinning, showing the majority of his impossibly straight teeth beneath a proud nose—like an Arab merchant having closed an agreeable sale in some Middle Eastern market. And he hadn't seemed at all surprised with the announcement, Max noted. *Randal must have already told him of the assignment.*

Gordon, on the other hand, had not turned from his task and appeared to barely make note of the news. He had paused—for perhaps a millisecond—in the assailing of his calculator's keys, but he'd remained hunched over his desk, his closely shorn blond head bent low over his workpapers ... as his ears reddened. The previous day, after they'd consumed the last of their brown-bag lunches at their desks, he'd informed the two of them, Max and Lou, that he expected to soon be leaving their shared space and midday repast—and the unending piles of tax returns—to begin the annual audit of Randal's largest client, VisualOptics Inc., a national eyeglass manufacturer and distributor. He'd allowed that, with the recent departure of Tom, one of the two senior auditors in the firm, he (with his two years of employment seniority over Max) was certain to be selected as Tom's replacement for the engagement. Thus, after having leaned far back in his chair and hooking his thumbs in the belt loops beneath his ample paunch, Gordon had opined that he was now positioned to "move up and out." In other words, he was due. But apparently Randal had other plans, as he'd just stated.

"Yeah," Randal was saying, "we'll swing by the new office and see how things are progressing. Then we'll swing over to Thirty-Fourth and drive up to Pinellas Park to meet with John Walton—he's the CEO—and Howard Fleet—he's the CFO ... but I guess you know that already." He stroked his chin and gazed out the room's single narrow window set high across the back wall, vacantly studying the alleyway behind the building as he talked. "Maybe we can meet them for lunch—on me—and talk about their year. Maybe get some internal financials from prior months. Maybe feel them out about last year's audit fee. Yeah ..."

Max stifled a snort. He was happy, and, from the corner of his eye, he'd glimpsed Lou unsubtly rolling his eyes: their boss was notorious for forgetting his wallet when lunches were to be "on him."

"And don't worry about bringing anything," Randal continued on, "except maybe a notepad. And, um … your calculator. Bring your calculator, Max. And your ruler—you'll need a ruler with the line template for the workpapers." Randal was old-school and liked seeing double wavy lines under the footed columns of numbers—and arrows, bright arrows, to direct your attention—and circled reference numbers, narrative blocks, and definite conclusions, boxed and neatly printed, on each and every grouping of audit workpapers. He had learned his auditing skills and techniques when he was with one of the big eight accounting organizations where knowing the firm's notational marks was almost as important as confirming the existence of the clients' major assets. "So that's all you'll need today. Maybe some Pentel lead: red, green, and black"—another audit preference of significance.

"What about a coffee cup?" Lou helpfully added. "Maybe an ashtray?"

"Well, they should have those—" Randal stopped midsentence when he realized he was being teased. "Yeah, you're right," he chuckled. "Just bring a notepad. You probably won't need supplies anyway until Monday when you're on-site. But, you know, maybe you should bring a pad, a six-column pad, just in case. And maybe some … oh, by the way. Would you guys mind working late tonight? I know it's sudden, but it's getting close to the six-fifteen filing deadline, and we still have a lot of returns to complete. And then we have extensions to prepare. So, OK … guys?" They nodded in unison without looking up.

• • •

Ten minutes later, Max slid in beside Minz, dropping onto the passenger's seat of the low-slung convertible, a glistening red affair, after having first deposited his calculator case and his heavy audit bag—now crammed with the prior year's workpaper files, three columnar pads, a roll of Scotch tape, a template ruler, an extra roll of calculator tape, and three tubes of Pentel leads of various colors—into the XKE's boot. Randal had retracted the car's roof so there was no space remaining behind the seats for his cases.

"So we're off," Randal declared, tentatively twisting the ignition key once, twice; the Jaguar's engine caught on the second try. "Whew," he breathed. He loved his car, but it could be quite troublesome at times to start. And he'd forgotten to bring from home the can of carb spray he'd sometimes resort to when the engine was exceptionally balky at starting. He gunned the motor and listened to the satisfying rumble. "We're off," he said again, as in affirmation, and slipped the car into gear. He eased down on the accelerator and steered from his reserved space in the paved parking area at the front of the building to the lot's exit and then to the west, down Central Avenue toward the Pasadena neighborhood and the new office building. The warming near-noon summer air immediately swallowed them, washing back over the windshield and buffeting them from side to side. He pressed down harder.

Max barely watched as the car gained speed, the structures and side streets now flicking by; he was still thinking about Gordon. After their boss had left the room, squeezing his way back down the long hallway to retrieve his jacket and sunglasses, Max had tried talking with his office mate. As he stocked his audit bag, he had tried to apologize to the big man, telling him he was sorry about the obviously disappointing announcement and promising his immediate consideration should there be need of additional assistance from the office. But the fellow would not be comforted; head down and crimson-eared, he'd continued to bang away at his calculator keys until Max had finally given up trying and left the room—"for a precautionary pit stop," he'd said. In his absence, Gordon had gotten to his feet and slipped out the back door "to get some lunch," he'd mumbled to Lou.

Well, there's nothing else I can do, Max told himself, still feeling irritation with the man's childish attitude. *Nothing else to do. Dang! It's hot out here already.* He settled back in the Jag's tight bucket seat (Colombian leather) and watched Randal synchronize his speed to the changing of the traffic signals. *I just hope the fat ass didn't spit in my coffee cup or something on his way out to get some lunch.* He remembered Lou once telling him that Gordon was a "strange sort of duck," and there had been that uncomfortable situation on his first day at work when the strange duck had switched out their calculators and desk chairs—old for new. "Pissing contest for silly accountants," Gene had opined when he'd visited the professor the next day before class at USF. But Max had not protested the theft back then ... to Gordon or Randal or anyone else—*when I should have*—and now he wondered if that might have been a big mistake, his not having stood up for himself. *Gordon's one of those passive-aggressive types ... who'll never be a friend anyway,* he decided. He'd known such people in the past.

And he can either respect me, he concluded, *or fear me.* From those past experiences with such people, he believed that only the observation of—or imposition of—mutual common respect (and maybe an added dash of fear of him) would allow them to effectively coexist in their future workplace. *Otherwise the guy'll continue to try to take advantage of me ... and we don't have to be buddies, do we?* He put aside his thoughts for the moment, resolving to try one more time to sit down with Gordon when they returned to the office later on this afternoon; for now, the new building was coming up fast on the left. His boss had covered the distance in record time.

Selecting a parking space at the edge of the pavement—"Far away from the building to avoid nails dropped by the carpenters," he'd said—Randal braked to a sliding stop, set the hand brake, and switched off the engine, and all was quiet except for the soft ticking of the cooling motor. "Nice ride, huh?" He flipped down his visor's mirror to check for wind damage to his dark slicked-back hair. "All good," he judged, now dabbing at his pencil-thin moustache. *And no gray showing ... but thinning on top, dammit!* Minz was exceedingly conscious of his appearance, and he was turning forty this year—an age, he'd once told his wife, Sarah, when they should be secure and free to travel. "Perhaps to Poland," he'd said, the country from whence Sarah's parents had fled prior to the Nazi invasion. "Or maybe even to Lebanon," the country of his parents' birth.

In the early 1900s, after Randal's folks had immigrated, settled in this new land, and reestablished connections with relatives, they'd done very well financially in the import-export trade. They had later relocated from New York to Florida, and Randal and his brother had enrolled in college. Randal had met Sarah there, in Miami at the U of M, where he'd chosen to major in accounting, "a pursuit more or less a hobby to a Jew, rather than an occupation," he'd told Max. The couple had married soon after graduation and, after another four years and Randal's employment stint with a regional CPA firm in Miami, moved back to New York, where he'd been fast-tracked to partnership with one of the big national firms. A decade then passed, and the couple returned to Florida—Saint Petersburg this time. Randal had bought Lou's tax-practice clientele and quickly expanded, collecting up those tax clients he'd kept in contact with over the years and new companies, primarily owned or operated by Jews: furniture stores, jewelers, physician practices, hospitals, synagogues, attorney practices, and so on. He'd also done well in attracting clients from the gentile community, where having a Hebrew as your accountant and tax adviser seemed to bestow a cachet unmatched by H&R Block. In summary, as he now neared the age of forty, Randal could be said to have prospered greatly.

"We'll go in the back and come out the front," he directed, easing shut the Jag's door and pushing in with his thigh. "Won't take a minute, and then we'll go meet John at that new seafood restaurant over on Nineteen North, past Thirty-Eighth Avenue."

But their excursion through the converted house took longer than Randal had anticipated: he'd had more than a few instructions for the plumbers and carpenters, pointing out many deficiencies for them to correct. However, for Max, it was all very enlightening—educational even. He saw another side of Randal, an away-from-the-office Randal. He watched and listened as they wandered from room to room and discovered Minz to be almost an actor, altering his script for the workman he was addressing: with one worker, he demanded; with another, he inquired; and with another, he cajoled. With all, he positively but imperceptibly led. *Was it conscious or contrived—something to be learned?*

"What are you grinning at?" Randal asked. They'd reached the front office space directly off the lobby and well away from the carpenters. He'd turned, waiting for Max to catch up.

"Well, Randal, that was pretty impressive," he chuckled. "Impressive."

"Meaning?"

"Well, not wanting to appear like some sort of kiss ass to you, I was impressed in there with the way you related to those workmen. I mean, you sounded like a good ol' boy with the trim guy—a trace of a Southern accent even. And with the guy cleaning up the scrap from the floors back there? You said something nice to him, and he wants to show you how neat he'd stacked the trash out back." Max laughed again. "You know, I'm not sure you realize how deftly you handled each of those guys—differently from back in the office with us accountants." *Maybe it's a talent you're born with, handling people? Maybe that's why he did so well in New York?*

Randal snorted. "Max, you make it sound like I'm ... like I'm manipulating people or something. Yeah, you may think they heard me and understood me—maybe even agreed with me—but you won't know until the work is done. Just the same, that's interesting—your observation—hadn't thought much about it. I suppose you've always got to talk with people in a way they can relate to you, at any level, from corporate boardrooms to your own front door. And you shouldn't have to talk down to people anywhere, I guess ... unless you see that's the only way they'll respond and do their jobs. These guys? I'm sure these men had their best client-faces on, too—for me. See? Ever work as a carpenter? I have. And carpenters will be the first to tell you that they'll tell their customers anything they think they'll want to hear ... just to get them to move on, to leave the worksite and get the hell out of the way. I mean they're really the experts in steering around customers, with presenting an agreeable appearance—maybe the best of all the trades ... excepting roofers, of course. Roofers are probably even better at it than anyone, and their screwups don't show up until they're long gone—and it rains. So, when you think about it, I guess it's basically a two-way street in all business relationships. Negotiations are always ongoing. In everything. All the time, when you think about it. You agree?"

Humility? "Yeah," Max agreed. "But, I mean, those guys were laughing and slapping you on the back while you were telling them that they'll have to work overtime to get the job done to your satis-faction. I mean, they sounded like they'd run through hell in gaso-line-soaked drawers for you right now."

"Hah! Think so? Hell? I dunno. Maybe they'll just do the best job they're capable of doing right now for me—that'd be enough for me. All the better if they do it because they want to. Regardless, I hope they're still around when it rains.

"By the way." Randal raised his arms and turned in place, chang-ing the subject. "By the way, this will be your office—your office only. Big enough for you, pal? What do you think of it? Want some-thing more done?"

Max looked about the room, for the first time. *Wood panel-ing. Pile carpeting. Wide window facing the road.* It was a much nicer office than he'd expected. *By myself?* Maybe it was his turn to be motivated. "You mean I won't be sitting in the big office back there?" That room, "with desk space for six," had been pointed out to him when they'd walked through the adjoining open area. "With the rest of the staff?"

Randal huffed again. "No, no. You're going to need some pri-vacy ... for the audit work and write-up management you'll be doing. I've got plans for you, boy."

Uh-oh. "Um, you know Gordon's got seniority on me and—"

"Don't worry about that, kiddo. I've got other plans for Gordon, and he's ... he doesn't have the aptitude for the work you'll be involved with. See? He wouldn't be happy for long. See, if a man doesn't have the abilities required for a job," he said, "the worst thing you can do is to put him in such a position; it'd only be a temporary thing. Understand? Give him something to do that he can excel at."

"Yeah," Max quietly replied. He believed he did understand: he'd been given a compliment of sorts. *So maybe I'm to be the one running through hell in gasoline-soaked drawers?* Regardless, he felt good, worthy to be confided in, relied on, professional. *Appreciated.*

They left the building through the front door and reboarded the Jag; its engine caught on the first try. Randal steered it from its parking space and back onto Central Avenue, heading fast to the east. After they'd traveled several blocks, Randal took note of his passenger's thoughtful demeanor. Leaning in close, he nudged with an elbow. "Trust me, Max," he yelled, competing with the exhaust pipes and the rushing winds. "Trust me," he affirmed, smiling and winking.

Max grimaced. His boss had also once told him that "trust me" meant "f*** you" in Yiddish.

"Hah!" Randal brayed, belly laughing as if he'd divined the same thought from Max's expression. "Trust me," he repeated.

Twenty minutes later, they pulled into another parking lot—this one freshly paved and striped. Selecting a spot beyond the valet drop-off area, well past the front door of the low, seemingly rustic building, Minz parked the vehicle and set its hand brake and then watched its fabric top ratchet shut overhead, clicking into the twin brackets above the windshield. He twisted the locks and dolefully announced, "We're here."

"Nice restaurant," Max observed, surveying about as he rose from the vehicle, gently closing his door using his butt and thigh.

At the front of the car, he noted, the towering queen palms—freshly installed at the pavement's edge—shaded them from the hot sun while a pair of appropriately rusted iron anchors, carefully positioned among the tree trunks, completed the staged and Caribbean-inspired motif. "Looks really pretty."

"Pretty damned expensive," Randal groused, slamming his door shut. He was already regretting his announced decision to pay the tab. "Maybe I'll suggest luncheon salads for the group?"

Uh-oh. Max pursed his lips to stifle a grin and began the trek to the building, putting on his jacket and picking up speed as he walked. He hurried with the hope that his boss wouldn't now call him back, summoning him to return to the car to lug his heavy audit bag into the impressive restaurant. He imagined he'd look like some kind of lackey straining under his load, wheezing to keep up with the fast-stepping Minz. *Twelve more steps to the door and—*

"Max! Max! You forgot all your stuff back there in the trunk!"

Damn. "Aw, Randal," he whined. "Can't I just come back out for that stuff if ... when I need it?"

"OK. OK. If you want to have to walk all the way back out here to get it ..." he conceded, grumbling and trudging on, head down, through the tastefully weathered wooden door Max held wide for him.

In the cool dimness of the restaurant, an attractive, lei-adorned hostess awaited them.

Randal halted. "Oh God!" he whispered. "This'll really be expensive! Maybe we could all drink water with our salads?"

"Mr. Minz?" she inquired. At his reluctant nod, she continued, "Mr. Walton and Mr. Fleet have already arrived and are having drinks in the Captain's Lounge while your table is being set. Please to follow me." She even sounded Polynesian. "The requested accommodations are so nice ... unusual for such small party. Very nice."

"Very expensive, you mean," he muttered, looking about. "Maybe we're not too late to get back out the door before—"

"Hey, Randal!" a voice boomed. It was too late.

"Well, hey, yourself, old man," Randal heartily greeted in return. Emerging from the bar's dark doorway, an enormous florid-complected man in a white dress shirt with tightly rolled sleeves ambled toward them, his smile wide, his broad hand extended. Firmly grasping the hand, Randal turned slightly to introduce Max standing at his side. "John, meet Max Anderson. He's to be your lead auditor this year."

The big man leaned forward and engulfed the young accountant's hand with his other massive paw. "Hey, bud," he greeted.

Whoa, thought Max. Randal had told him John Walton was a large fellow, a former football player, once a lineman at the University of Florida, but, to him, this guy was well past simply being large. "Eh … howdy," he stammered in reply.

"Glad to meetcha, son. Anderson, huh? I've met a few of those. Come from up above Atlanta maybe?"

Max was instantly a friend of Walton's. He'd heard from Randal how the man had managed to put together his multimillion-dollar company in a hostile business climate and to turn out record profits year after year with an unusually loyal workforce, and now the guy appeared to, well—to genuinely like him. *This is a good person.* Max could sense it. "Glad to meet you, too, sir," he responded— and really meant it.

"Sir?" the big man questioned, as if taken aback. "Sir? That's not me; that's my daddy … and I'd say you weren't born much farther north than, say, Kentucky, with those manners. So how 'bout just calling me John, son? I don't look that much older 'n you, do I?"

"Yes, sir, and, eh, no, sir," Max readily agreed—and agreed— smiling in return. Randal had also told him of the CEO's penchant for ferreting out a person's history and personal attributes, in addition to birth origins. John himself was a true Floridian and was one of the few Saint Petersburg residents who'd actually been born in Pinellas County. More than a half century earlier, he'd been delivered in Bayfront Medical Center down on the south side. The hospital had then been called Mound Park, having been named for the nearby Indian shell mound. *John may be a lot older than me but he's definitely well-preserved. That's some grip!*

Another man, equally tall but thin, swarthy, and stylishly suited, sauntered into the reception area, also coming from the direction of the lounge. He held a cocktail glass in his hand and used it to affect a raised, casual salute. "Hello, Randal," he greeted, his voice flat.

"Hello, Howard," Randal replied, his voice likewise low—and guarded.

The pause grew long, and Max decided he should make his own introduction to the CFO; the pair reminded him of a couple of alley cats on a back fence, sizing up each other for the scuffle sure to follow. *Don't need that.* Extending his now-freed hand, he cheerfully addressed the other: "Good afternoon, Mr. Fleet. I'm Max Anderson, and I'll be assisting this year with the audit." *After all,* he reasoned, *I'll be the one who'll have to work with this guy.*

Fleet regarded Max's outstretched hand much as he would a turd on a stick and passed on the opportunity to grasp the proffered member. "Hello," he acknowledged, again slightly raising his cocktail glass, deigning to exhibit the least possible interest in this young man. After all, he'd seen staff auditors come and go; "God-awful nuisances," he'd say, mere irritants in his daily guidance of VisualOptics. In fact, just this past week, he'd twice approached Walton with requests for the board's consideration of other auditing groups for this year's attestation, of their possible favoring of other accounting firms with reputations in the industry equivalent in importance to their company's—firms like Price Waterhouse and E&E, one of his former employers in Chicago. "Now those are names that would lend gravitas to our financial statements," he had argued. But the CEO would not be persuaded, calling Minz one of the finest accountants he'd ever known. "Sharp," he'd said, adding that as long as he had an opinion, and a vote, Randal Minz, CPA, PA, would remain VisualOptics' first and only auditor.

John Walton had engaged Minz's accounting firm when he'd first begun operations in the city, opening his initial manufacturing facility in a high-windowed warehouse down on the south side of town. He'd hired the CPA to advise him on the setting up of the company's accounting books and procedures and had requested that the man stay on to assist with the preparation of documentation relating to his company's financing needs. Randal had early on impressed John in various ways but especially so on that one day, after his having witnessed the CEO signing the tall stacks of checks the secretary customarily deposited on his desk: the CPA had waited until John was on the phone and then slipped in a check of his own, about halfway down one pile. Then, later, while John was pooh-poohing the accountant's latest entreaty for improved internal controls ("Unnecessarily expensive for the company's efficient operations," he'd said), Randal had produced the signed check with a flourish: $1,000,000 payable on demand to Randal Minz, CPA, PA. They'd bonded that day. Walton generally liked and trusted people and worked best with people who liked and trusted him in return. But for those who'd prove to not be so trustworthy, he'd need people like Minz around, who'd look out for him and his fledgling company.

As time had passed and VisualOptics' operations had continued to prosper, expanding throughout the Florida market and beyond, John and his team were forced to move their major manufacturing operations north a few miles to Pinellas Park, where they'd constructed a huge laboratory and warehouse complex to service the rising national demand for their principal product: precision-ground ophthalmic lenses. And more recently, while working with an augmented team of scientists and engineers, they'd hit upon a process for making soft contacts that promised to revolutionize the industry, producing durable lenses at a fraction of what they then cost. He and his company were indeed on the cusp of even greater successes. However, these continuing opportunities had created still more fiscal needs, which generally revolved around coupling their world-class marketing future with a world-class financing capacity. For that, they'd decided, VisualOptics should go public. And for that, they'd need a verifiably reported financial history—Minz's annual audits—and competent, specialized leadership—Howard Fleet's high-finance experience. That was the way the company had to go, John and his team had decided, because that was where the real money resided—along with their futures.

Max studied the CFO's face. When it became apparent Fleet was not to take his hand, he allowed his arm to slowly drop to his side, all the while hoping his flushed-faced embarrassment went unnoticed by the other men; he had felt the heat rising in his neck. *Damn guy looks like a snake anyway, like some mafia character.* His initial awed impression of the slick, well-dressed officer had vanished, becoming a rouged shape in a haze of anger that, in turn, was immediately stilled, chilled, and clarified: he would not—could not—allow this man to determine his response, to control him in any way. "So, Howard," he continued, casual-like, now using the other's first name, now rationing his own respect in turn, "Mr. Minz has told me much about you"—he really hadn't said anything about him—"and I'd imagine you're somewhat dismayed. You'd have preferred to see Tom again this year to minimize any learning curves … but, I promise you, I'll have thoroughly reviewed the prior year's audit work papers before Monday morning. I'll arrive at nine o'clock sharp." *Enough said. Left him nothing to approve.* He stepped back. He'd worked with such men before—supervisors and officers in private industry and NCOs and officers in the military; he judged Fleet to be as self-centered and arrogant as any of them. He scrutinized the CFO for any reaction.

The dark man's features showed only minor confusion. "Who's Tom?" he finally asked.

"Tom was Randal's senior auditor last year," John answered, inserting himself into the conversation. He'd witnessed Fleet needlessly ignoring the young man; he had seen him do it with others. And it always embarrassed him that the man, a member of his team, his business family, could be so dismissive of someone he'd apparently deemed subordinate to himself. *But that's the way people treat each other where Howard's from,* he reasoned—his standard rationale. He made a mental note to stop by the auditor's desk on Monday morning after the young man had arrived and fill him in on his CFO's idiosyncrasies. He'd done the same with Tom last year, explaining that though the man was short on courtesy, he'd made up for it with his obvious intellect and experience in the corporate world, and John was certain they'd especially value Howard for the job ahead, when the company had publicly issued stock and was competing on the international stage. He'd tell Max of the interim bond financing Fleet had put in place and how he'd already proven his connections in the nation's industries: on their "road show," Howard had introduced him to men whose names he'd actually remembered seeing in the pages of *Forbes* and *Businessweek*; he'd never expected to meet them in person. "Yes," he'd say to Max, "they'll need Fleet for the future." So for now, they'd work around the guy's personality ... and the auditors would just have to understand.

"Would you gentlemens please to follow me?" the beautiful hostess requested in her lovely, sing-song manner. Three of the four men silently breathed their relief for the interruption; Howard Fleet was still thinking, trying to recall Tom from the prior year's audit.

• • •

Two hours later, Max stood outside the Jag, waiting for his boss to unlock his door from the inside. *Click.* Tugging the handle and pulling the door wide, he dropped onto the low seat. "Jeez, Randal, what a jerk!" he immediately opined, now certain he couldn't be overheard outside the car. "Did you hear how Fleet talked to that waitress? That bastard almost had her crying. I'm surprised she'd even come back to the table for the—hey!" He paused. "Hey, I thought you were buying today. Wasn't that John Walton's American Express card on the tab?"

"He beat me to it, kiddo," Randal muttered, flipping through the keys on his ring. "He'd probably told the waitress to bring the bill directly to him and not to me. I tried to pay—you saw me."

"Outfumbled you, huh?" Max teased, putting aside his indignation with Fleet for the moment. "Got bruises all over your bod where you were beating your pockets, huh? Well, those'll probably heal in a day or two, I bet. Probably just glancing blows anyway," he added.

Randal sent a quick sideways glare his way—a well-practiced gesture that concealed his true feeling: satisfaction. He'd just dodged a sizable luncheon tariff; he was happy.

"Kidding, just kidding," Max soothed. "I'm just picking at you. Anyway, the girl seemed to have brightened up considerably when she retrieved her little payment tray."

"Yeah," Randal agreed, now turning in his seat and checking around the sides and back of the automobile. "John has always been especially considerate of the waitstaff—as he is to almost everyone." He inserted the selected key and turned it once, twice; the motor caught on the third try. "Whew!" he breathed as he goosed the engine a couple of strokes, watching the tachometer needle respond. "Good. Now, what were you saying—oh, you were saying she's OK with her tip? Yeah, John is always solicitous with the waitstaff; he told me he'd once waited tables." Randal slipped the car into gear and slowly eased from the parking place, backward and then forward, turning the Jag's wire-rimmed wheels and aiming its long nose toward the second of two exits. With another momentary shoe tap and the vehicle's virtual response—a powerful swell hinting of acceleration potential—he allowed the little car to coast forward, smoothly, silently, as its roof retracted again into the tight space behind the two seats.

"No, no, it's more than that—more than his having worked as a waiter," Max insisted. "When I worked as a busboy, when I was still in high school, I'd noticed that a lot of the powerful and most wealthy looking people were especially gracious to the servers like, you know, when you'd see them out having dinner. I think most great men and women are like that: considerate with the people who are doing the jobs that some people could choose to look down on. Like Fleet," he added, recalling his own embarrassment.

Randal's lips tightened, and he shook his head. "Yeah, exactly like Howard Fleet all right—he's a horse's ass, isn't he?" he growled. "By the way, when you're out there Monday, try to stay away from the guy as much as possible. Last year, he'd call me daily to complain about Tom's asking stupid questions or whatever—bothering him—complaints like that. I'm surprised he couldn't recall Tom's name; he sure bitched enough about him."

"How'd Tom handle that?"

"Primarily by avoiding Howard as much as he could. Tom was thoroughly intimidated by the man; he hated asking any questions or even talking with him. So, he'd saved up his questions for me to ask when I came out in the final week." Minz twisted in his seat, checking the traffic flow coming south on US 19 before pressing forward, merging the Jag into a long opening. "But that also made the last week very hectic," he noted, raising his voice to make himself heard over the passing wind.

"Is that what you want me to do? Wait for you?" Max asked, also raising his voice. "Or maybe I should talk with John if I have questions?"

Randal stared ahead, thoughtful. "Well, I guess you could, if you thought it would be something he'd know about. Maybe for board-of-directors questions. Probably not for financial statements though. What I'm saying is just don't let Fleet intimidate you like he did Tom. You know, I sometimes worry that the lad took shortcuts in certain places in the audit program ... because he was afraid to ask the tough questions."

Max assumed his own thoughtful expression. "You mean like he faked responses on the audit program? Maybe shaded his conclusions?"

"Well, it happens, my boy—the lesser of disturbing, painful alternatives. But just don't get yourself into such a position. Maybe do the big stuff, verifying assets and liabilities on the balance sheet first ... confirmations ... and do your ticking and tying in the final week when I'm there." Randal gunned the Jag to weave in and around a slower car ahead; he was exceeding the speed limit by almost twenty miles per hour. "I mean, what can he do if he does get pissed at you?"

"Kill and eat me?" Max laughed. They were both yelling now.

"Well, I doubt he'd care to eat you ... unless you're expensive ... and French."

• • •

Arriving back at the office, Max made a great show of extracting himself from the low-slung Jaguar, grunting and pulling himself erect against the car's door, all for his boss's benefit. "Jeez, Randal," he groaned. "Why don't you buy yourself a real car? Something where you don't have to step down in order to get inside. Something American! Something built in the colonies!"

Minz, totally unsympathetic, ignored the taunts and pressed his door shut. "Why don't you just get some exercise, boy? You're wheezing like Lou—no, worse than Lou. He, at least, owns a gym membership." Walking around to the rear of the car, he flicked out his pocket handkerchief, using it to scatter the imaginary grains of dust befouling the gleaming red surface of the car. "You're not even—what?—thirty?"

Max thought before answering, his brow furrowed. "Twenty-six," he muttered. "And I don't get any exercise because you make me work twelve hours a day, seven days a week. And that reminds me, Mr. Minz: when are you going to pay our overtime? Maybe I could afford a gym membership then." He'd actually wanted to broach the pay issue for the last couple of weeks, since Lou had told him of Randal's method of paying overtime: accumulating the overtime hours and paying in lump sums. Lou had said the practice was called Chinese overtime and was beneficial to the employer because after a certain number of hours had accumulated in the pool, those additional hours became payable at the straight hourly wage rate and not at the time-and-a-half rate. He'd said that very few employers used that method because very few people knew it was available under wage and hour regulations. "Leave it to ol' Randal," he'd said to Lou. "If anyone would know about a loophole in taxes, he'd be the one." Last week, his boss had pointed out to him another little-known exemption in the regs regarding the nonliability of payroll taxes on the wages of children employed by their parents in a family business. And, of course, Randal Minz, CPA, PA, happened to have a number of clients who'd employed their kids in their family businesses—even when those children were attending schools in distant states. *Great way to deduct your kids' allowances, I guess.*

Using his handkerchief to avoid finger marks, Randal thumbed open the Jag's boot and reached inside for the audit bag. Grabbing its handle, he jerked it up and out, setting it heavily onto the asphalt. "Well, my boy," he began, now straightening and brushing his hands with the well-used cloth, "it is about time to—arrrgh!" He grabbed at the small of his back with both hands.

"What's that?"

"Arrrgh!" Randal repeated.

"Aw, come on," Max replied, as unsympathetic as his boss. "It can't be that painful to have to pay overtime and—"

"Oh! Oh! Oh! It's my spine, Max! I hurt it lifting your damn case out of the boot! Damn, that thing's heavy! Why'd you bring it anyway?" Randal demanded. He looked up then and glimpsed the younger man's face, reddening as he rounded the vehicle—but still coming to his assistance.

"Randal—"

"Never mind, never mind … but thanks. Thanks," he groaned, refusing any aid, his one hand uplifted. "I'll be OK. I guess—eh—never mind. I'll just mosey on—ouch!" Remaining in this bent posture, with both hands pressed to his lower back, Randal shuffled on by Max and toward the building's entrance. He avoided raising his head to meet the other's eyes a second time.

"Eh, Randal?" Max persisted, raising his voice to be heard. "Maybe we can talk about the overtime … later?"

"Can you just catch the trunk lid, son?" Randal called back over his shoulder. He'd reached the building and entered by the front door, disappearing down the long hallway without a single backward glance.

"Wow! All that over paying overtime?" Max wondered aloud, watching the glass door stutter shut. "So I guess it'll be a while before I get a gym membership. Or maybe ol' Randal really did hurt his back just now." He lowered the trunk lid, listening for the latch to click. His disappointment and irritation faded with that latter thought. "Maybe he really did. And, anyway, I guess I've gotten a promotion of sorts today ... son."

Another thought then came to him: "Gordon!" He should go check his car before he went inside; he'd meant to do it earlier—before he'd left to go with Randal. "A passive-aggressive guy could do real damage to an automobile's finish ... with a little ol' key," he quietly observed. In fact, Gordon had once told him of his own car getting "keyed" in a bar's parking lot because he'd stolen another guy's girlfriend. Max had doubted that the overweight, nearsighted accountant had, in fact, ever stolen anyone's girlfriend, but he'd never doubted the man's experience with the revenge tactic. *That'd be exactly something he's capable of doing if he's pissed off at me. And he did sneak out the back door when I'd gone to the bathroom.* Max hefted the audit bag and hurried around the side of the long, low building to search for his vehicle in the back parking area.

He found the lot packed with cars, primarily those of owners employed by the other businesses renting office space in the building, but he quickly located his own, the aging Chevy on the back row. He performed a cursory inspection and determined that his paint job remained intact, unscathed—except for a couple of rust spots. But Gordon had nothing to do with those; the spots had been there when he'd bought the Chevrolet years before.

And now he felt somewhat guilty ... that he'd suspected his coworker of being capable of such a nefarious, vengeful action. *Maybe I should do something nice for him—maybe take him to* lunch. "I bet that fat boy would appreciate a meal at someone else's expense." *Great idea.* But he'd better first check his funds before asking. *Payday's still a ways off.*

Entering their accounting office through the rear door, Max carefully made his way down the box-jammed corridor, turning in at the first door to his left: their three-desk, shared quarters. Lou and Gordon were still hunched over their desks, working away at their respective clients' tax returns. He dropped the audit bag to the floor. *Whomp!* No one turned with the noise; they'd heard him coming in the back.

"Did Minz buy lunch?" Lou inquired.

"No."

"Figures. Mr. Moore wouldn't bet with me that he would. ... Say, didn't we have a bet on it? You and I?"

Max laughed. "Nooo. You know I wouldn't have taken that bet with you either, Lou. Like him." Gordon grunted his amusement without turning; he was listening.

So, are you gonna ask him if he'll eat lunch with you tomorrow? Now's the time, boy. Max cleared his throat. "Hey, Gordon, my man. Gordon ... umm." His eyes passed over his own desktop ... and the thirteen-column workpaper pad he'd left lying there. The pad's top page, the one containing the final calculations of the extensive depreciation schedule he'd prepared for Mr. Jason W. Wilson's Form 1040, Schedule C, was gone! *Dang! I promised Mr. Wilson he'd have his tax return by tomorrow at the latest—so the man could go on vacation!* Flipping open the thick manila folder beside the pad, Max saw that several more pages had been removed from the inside clip—all those schedules that had taken him hours and hours to calculate and complete. With his thoughts already biased, predisposed, he rushed to judgment—and white-hot anger rushed back: *Gordon Moore!*

Silence. A full minute ticked by while he stood there, staring at the empty columnar page and thinking his thoughts: *Spiteful! What've I ever done to him? Could he have really done this?*

Because of Randal's choice? Max was trying to fathom an act that he wouldn't have imagined. *No reason!* he finally decided. *Just out-and-out … mean!* This conclusion would make little sense to him later, but he felt some satisfaction now, and later, he'd think more. But, at this moment, he also needed to think about breathing again. *Blow. Slow. Even. Control.* More time passed before he could trust himself to talk.

Meantime, the other two accountants continued at their respective tasks, their blank backs to him. *And Gordon hasn't responded to me calling his name. Hasn't moved. He knows what I'm seeing.* "Um, Mr. Moore?" he croaked, and coughed. He waited. "Gordon, do you know what's happened to my depreciation schedules?" he asked again, his tone now hard, serious.

Moore continued working, scribbling on the papers on his desk, leaning forward with his legs tucked back under his chair. As usual, his white shirttail had escaped his trousers in the back, and his boxer underwear was showing above his belt. "Mr. Wilson's tax schedules?" he finally replied nonchalantly, not bothering to glance over—a question in return.

"Yeah."

"No."

Max sighed heavily. His head hurt. He wanted so much to slap the glasses from the man's fat face.

Across the room, Lou rotated about in his chair to face them. "Why?" he asked. "Can't find 'em or something?" He stood and walked over, to stand beside Max. He lifted the pad from the desk, flipped through the remaining blank pages, and asked additional questions, showing his concern: "Could you have filed them? Taken them with you? Put them in a drawer? …"

Max replied no to each well-meaning inquiry.

"After you'd left … and Gordon was still gone," Lou mulled, "and I believe I'd stepped out awhile for lunch. … Sooo, I dunno. But, if I was just guessing …" The old man's voice lingered on the last syllable, drawing it long. He lifted his eyes to Max's and slightly, briefly, tilted his head toward Gordon's broad back; he likewise had suspicions.

Max understood—perfectly. *Shit! At least I won't be buying Gordon a damn meal now.* He sighed heavily again and eased himself onto his squeaky chair, to begin working on new depreciation schedules. It was a good thing he'd ordered big at lunch today, he thought. *I'll be working late tonight.*

• • •

At a quarter past three in the morning, Max let himself out the back door, rattling the knob behind to make sure the lock had caught. The moon was full; from the back stoop, he could see his old Biscayne in the far parking area, standing lonely and forlorn. *Not another car in the lot.*

"Well, it took a while, but ol' Wilson should be pleased with the results," he told himself, talking aloud as he stepped down to the pavement. Since he'd previously completed the same schedules and was more aware of tax outcomes, he'd taken the opportunity to change a few depreciation methods here and there and had expensed a few more assets with the second preparation, causing Mr. Wilson's net taxable income to drop to a lower bracket. *Barely.* "It's just a period deferral, but at least the man should be less apt to complain about his bill this year. Hah! That's another thing ol' Randal's good at: billing." He began to whistle as he walked, having put aside the anger he'd felt earlier when he discovered the missing workpapers. He was satisfied with his efforts, and he was happy to be heading home. "What a day, what a day. Good thing I've only got plants at home to water. Don't think another person could stand me—"

Midstride, he stopped: He'd noticed something different about his car. *Scratches!* "Friggin' scratches!" The long lines crisscrossed the dark paint on his rear quarter panel and shined in the moonlight. *Shining like they were made by a rake.* "That asshole! That damn Moore!" Despite earlier suspecting—and voicing—the capability of the man to commit such a cowardly act, he now realized he didn't understand anything at all. "Just out-and-out low shit!" That conclusion was no longer satisfying in the least. "You just don't do this to a car! My car!" He realized now that he'd delayed—and he'd made another mistake: he'd again said nothing to the fat boy when he had the chance. He had just calmed himself and said nothing at all.

"But you doubted *yourself*, didn't you, and thought you needed more proof before accusing Moore of taking your workpapers, didn't you?" After he had returned in the late afternoon, he'd decided he would wait until Lou was out of the office before confronting Gordon. But the man had slipped out early, through the rear door, leaving for the day without saying anything further to either him or Lou.

"Just up and left without saying a word, dammit! I should've at least followed him out and waited for him to leave—" *But would you want to do that every day?* "No, I wouldn't." He realized that would have only been a temporary fix, and a temporary solution was essentially no solution. "No, I don't want to have to continually watch my back. I want him to respect me!" *But with some people, if there's no fear, there's no respect.* "It's the same thing to those people. And that's the way it is with Moore. Without him respecting me, this'll happen again and again. You know, I should get in the car right now and drive over to his house and—*but you're not thinking clearly, are you, Max?* That thought could have come from outside himself … and it was true. He *was* out of control. He could hear his blood pounding in his ears; he could feel the heat behind his eyeballs.

He leaned back against his car. "You need to breathe, boy. You need to calm yourself. You've had a long day." *Yeah, almost twenty-four hours of day.* "And just what do you think you can do now that you can't do later … and maybe won't regret later?" He felt the heat gradually receding from behind his forehead. A second thought flitted by: *Or is this what you did earlier, when you wanted to talk to him in private? Are you afraid of Gordon?* Max shook his head. "I'm gonna go home. Sleep on it. And tomorrow think of something else … something motivational." It had been years since he'd had to threaten another person. *Can I do it?*

About two hours later, when the horizon was just beginning to lighten with the new day, Max managed to drift off into fitful sleep, a dream-filled slumber involving vague images—large buildings, dark rooms, and long-forgotten faces—and vivid emotions—confusion, fear, and anger. But only a single dream, a memory, would remain with him when he wakened later in the morning—about an event that had happened years before, back during his basic training days at Lackland Air Force Base in Texas.

• • •

He remembered that the bunk beside his own had been reassigned to a new airman basic, who'd belatedly joined their class—a routine-type flight in a regular-type squadron—after having spent several weeks in another squadron, a "motivation flight" as it had then been known. Such nonroutine flights were one of two remedial programs designed by the Air Force for newly enlisted personnel adjudged as requiring additional attention before graduation—or rejection—from basic military training. The "fat boy flight" was for the overweight or physically deficient troops, while the motivation flight was for the undisciplined or mentally unstable airmen. With the selective service's draft then in effect and with recruiters still struggling to meet their Vietnam-bound quotas, the various militaries were loath to release any of their charges without at least attempting redemption. And Anwain Thacker, the new transferee, had been one of the redeemed.

Thacker was escorted to his new dormitory residence one afternoon when Max and his fellow trainees were engaged in the reassembling of their lives and laundry, after having endured the character-building exercise called a surprise inspection. That activity usually encompassed an unannounced, rampaging onslaught of about a half-dozen training instructors from the other squadrons; their destructive rummages through the airmen's drawers and lockers in search of misaligned seams and mis-spaced clothing; and their subsequent cuffs and curses when the airmen inevitably failed to measure up to some elusive criteria. Max remembered he'd just returned from retrieving his T-shirts and skivvies from a toilet bowl (a stray hair had been discovered in a fold of fabric, and, thus, the lot required immediate rewashing) when Thacker was marched in and made to stand at attention while Tech Sergeant Burke, their flight's TI, lectured the new troop on what was to be expected of him during the remaining weeks of training.

Max was initially impressed by the tall very-black young man standing there at the side of his bunk, seemingly absorbing Tech Sergeant Burke's instructions with rapt interest and smartly coming to attention when the sergeant turned to go. Then, to the TI's receding back, he gave a second salute—a salute of two fists, each with a finger fully extended high in the air. "Whoa!" Max had breathed. To his mind, the sergeant wasn't such a bad guy with the new troops, his charges. An older-than-usual businesslike noncom, he hadn't abused the recruits as many of the other TIs had done ... and enjoyed doing. He was fair and honest with the men and, from the start, very clear about his expectations of them. And they had responded in like fashion, their flight #1503 having become the goal setter for the other flights.

"That's not necessary," Max had commented to another airman standing nearby, "and I bet that's why that dude made the behavior flight." He'd turned away in disgust ... and Anwain Thacker noticed. The man had heard the disapproving comment and instantly marked Max as his enemy. That evening, after he'd openly filched the "white boy's" deodorant from his open locker, Thacker loudly threatened to beat his ass if Max dared complain about the theft.

Forced to review his options, Max soon determined he had few choices and, obviously, no physical ones—the big man was simply too large and muscular for that. He would have to be patient, he decided. "Maybe somehow we could be friends," he had hopefully remarked to his neighbor on the other side, a lanky boy from Louisiana who called himself Coon Ass.

The following morning, Thacker helped himself to a pair of Max's clean socks and, on the noon break, crashed heavily onto Max's carefully made cot to avoid messing up the covers of his own bed.

"Ain't much that ol' boy be understanding," Coon Ass had said. "You be soon attractin' attention from his frin's, too." He nodded toward the dayroom and the two troops standing there, talking and smoking with Thacker. "So you may be awanting to borrow dis maybe." He fished an eight-inch switchblade from under the metal cap of his bedpost. "Utterwise he make your life plumb miserable. Respect," he'd declared, tapping the side of his nose with a long forefinger.

"An astute observation," Max had replied. That night, after the midnight watch had passed and the snores and whimpers from the double rows of sleeping men were the only sounds in the bay, he'd slipped the knife from under his bedsheet and lifted it high overhead to study its profile against the ceiling tiles as he lay in his bunk. He pressed the button on the handle. *Snick.* The long thin blade flicked out and gleamed with red light reflected from the emergency exit lamps spaced along the walls. Instantly the breathing sounds abated in the neighboring bunks, their occupants awake and waiting, listening to the darkness.

"Anwain Thacker," Max had said in the silence, holding aloft the knife, turning it from side to side, as if marveling at its lethal length. He knew then he had the big man's full attention because, with a slight roll of his head to his left, he clearly saw two enormous white eyes off in the dimness. "Thacker," he'd begun again, keeping his voice low and husky and spacing his words, "maybe tonight I'll cut off your nose when you fall asleep ... or maybe your pecker if you don't wake up fast enough. You know you got to sleep sometime, don't you?" Max allowed quiet seconds to pass before resuming, all the while fighting an urge to bray with laughter at the sight of the open, unblinking eyes. "Your choice, Thacker. Leave me alone from now on, or when you fall asleep … *whack!*" He then clicked shut the blade and rolled over, away from Anwain. He heard no following sounds of quick movement or the shifting of weight on bedsprings—just the gradual resumption of the snores and grunts normal to the sleeping dormitory bay. Later on, about daybreak, Max roused and turned to his other side, to face Thacker; the big man's eyes were still open and staring. *Respect.*

Still later, by noon of the same day, Airman Thacker had traded bunks, moving himself around to the dorm's other bay and far away from Max.

• • •

"Anwain Thacker," Max said again, now staring at the ceiling in his own bedroom. He'd woken with a start—and a headache—after having slept for barely three hours. He was still very tired.

And he hadn't particularly enjoyed his memory of Airman Thacker. "What the heck's he got to do with … oh yeah." *Maybe he does relate to those scratches in my car's paint.* He mentally felt the rough gouges again; he could almost see the sparkle of dark paint flecks on his fingertips as he held his hand high in the morning sunlight. "Crap!"

Rolling to his side and swinging his feet to the floor, he sat on the side of the bed to think more about the dream. While he couldn't remember what had happened to Thacker after that day, as best as he could now recall, the remainder of their basic-training stint had been rather unremarkable; he and the other troops had graduated four weeks later and shipped out to air force bases across the country for still more training.

"So would ol' Gordon respond to a threat of castration?" he wondered aloud and then snorted at the thought. "He'd probably just call the cops on me. Ah well." He breathed deeply and pushed to his feet.

"So, it's the weekend. I'll drop off Mr. Wilson's return today, and on Monday, I'll be at VisualOptics. I won't have to do anything until three or four weeks from now. Maybe I'll have an idea by then. Maybe." *But at least I did something way back then.*

• • •

Monday dawned.

Slumped low in his parked car, Max sipped hot coffee and watched the employees arrive for work at the Pinellas Park facility. Several of the men passing between the cars slowed their stride alongside his Chevy. *Bet they're examining Gordon's artwork as they go by.* One of the men made a tsking sound with his tongue and commented to his companions. *Spanish. Sounds like sympathy anyway. They're shaking their heads.* He nodded in return, acknowledging the gestures; they added weak smiles of commiseration.

He'd arrived early this morning to observe the taking of VisualOptics' inventory and to make some test counts on his own, a standard auditing procedure. Last night Randal Minz had said he would probably drive over after lunch to help him with the counts and to gather up copies of the count sheets, saying that, if Francisco could break free, he would also come over to help with the count confirmations. Francisco Valdez, a senior auditor—their only senior auditor now that Tom had left—was working on his own audit at the nearby Morganton Yacht Company. "I'd think the counting of forty-foot-long boats," Randal had joked during their phone conversation, "should certainly take less time than the counting of glass slugs." Max had cautiously laughed in reply; he had no idea what a glass slug was.

Hey! He sat erect in the car seat, having spotted John Walton walking briskly along the sidewalk at the front of the main building. "Well, now's the time find out what that slug looks like," he grunted, pushing down on the clamped vise grip that functioned as his door handle. He had hoped the CEO would arrive early so he could avoid another embarrassing encounter with Howard Fleet.

Parking his now-empty cup on the passenger-side floor, he pushed wide his door and levered himself from the car. Opening the rear door, he yanked his audit bag and calculator case from off the backseat, closed both doors with his butt, and double-timed it across the warming asphalt, trying to reach the central entrance doors ahead of Walton.

"Good morning, sir," he puffed, still ten yards away.

"Good morning to you, Max," Mr. Walton greeted. "Remember now—just John."

Wow! Max was astonished the man had remembered their prior conversation *and* his name. "Well, OK then. So, good morning ... John." The accountant beamed his pleasure, and the CEO smiled back.

"Hey, I noticed you parked way over there," Max continued, pointing with a tilt of his head, "and not right here." He glanced over to the reserved parking spaces at the curb.

"Oh, that's just something Howard wanted—his own space. I think he's afraid someone will crash a car door into his Mercedes in the employees' parking area," he explained. "Or else he doesn't like the exercise. Ever think, Max, how some people will pay good money to a gym to walk for hours on a machine but wouldn't think twice of walking across a parking lot or mowing their own grass?"

Max nodded; he'd often thought about it. "You mow your lawn?" he asked.

"Well, nooo," John admitted, chuckling softly. "You got me, son. See, I would, but my wife wants it done during daylight hours—and not on a Sunday afternoon. Say, you married? Got a yard?"

"No and no."

"Stay that way. And when you get a house, you can let the grass grow clear up to your ... butt. You a religious man, Max?"

It was the auditor's time to laugh: "I'm a Christian, John—but not that easily offended—if that's what you mean. Telling me about getting your ass out of a ditch on a Sunday afternoon doesn't bother me a bit."

"Hah!" John huffed. "I think it was an ox in the Bible, Max, and not an ass … but there was a ditch involved." He playfully rapped the accountant's shoulder with the back of his hand. "See," he went on, explaining again, "I don't like offending people need-lessly or stepping on toes when I don't have to—and I don't like seeing other folks doing it. And speaking of toes, I wanted to tell you something—I'm glad we got this chance to talk; I wanted to catch you first thing. See, Howard worked in Chicago and New York before he started working here; he's from there. I expect Randal must have told you that already. Anyway, I wanted to warn you that people working in such high-powered financial markets in that neck of the woods may be a bit brisker with their words than we're used to down here. So try not to take offense because—"

"I'm OK, John," Max interrupted. "I'm OK. Randal filled me in … that is, if you're thinking that I maybe got my feelings hurt or something at lunch last week."

"Yeah, yeah. Well, I guess I saw you get a bit rust colored when … never mind."

"I'm turning red now?"

"Yeah. Pinkish, I'd say. But don't worry. The ladies will think it's charming, Fleet won't notice, and the Mexicans don't care. Blush all you want around here, son," John chuckled again, motioning the accountant forward with one hand and pulling wide the glass entrance door with the other. "So Randal has already talked with you? Good. Now, if you got questions—when you get questions—feel free to come talk to me about them. I might know a thing or two. Hah!" He gave a final shoulder rap. "So come on in here, boy, and get yourself settled in that first office over there to your right. The desk is open, and the phone works fine. Dial nine to get out. And if you want coffee, just tell this lovely lady here." A beauti-ful blond-haired woman joined them at the door. "This here's Nell, Max. She's my assistant and keeps my schedule straight. She can help with some of the answers, too, I bet." He grinned over at her. "Thanks, Nell."

"Hi," croaked Max. He was having difficulty maintaining eye contact with the young lady. *That's gotta be the tightest dress I've ever seen! Her boobs look ready to bubble out!*

"Hello," she greeted evenly, seemingly oblivious to such rapt attention. She added a tight, professional smile and nod as she handed several typed pages to the CEO. After he'd scribbled his signature on each page, she abruptly turned and strode smartly back across the wide reception area, her exceptionally high heels clicking on the hard terrazzo flooring. Both men watched until she reached the carpeted area before the executive offices. Nell had indeed been blessed in the physical way.

"Whoo," puffed John.

"Whoo," seconded Max. "Mighty fine ambulation there. She's attached?" he asked.

John slowly pivoted in place. He studied the accountant for several long, silent seconds.

"What?" Max blurted, his voice raised and his face cherry red. "Something I shouldn't have said? Hey! Listen! I'm not sexist, and I don't intend on asking her out and—"

"Hah!" John chortled in delight, interrupting the other's impassioned defense while, at the same time, patting the air in the space between them, making small tone-it-down hand motions. "That's OK, that's OK," he calmed. "I understand. That's OK. I'm just having a little fun with you." He continued to grin, obviously pleased with himself.

Max managed an uncertain smile in return. "Gosh, I thought I'd violated some—"

"Rule." John finished his sentence. "Sorry about that, boy. Actually, we don't have a lot of rules here. We're pretty casual day to day. But, having said that, we do have a few, and these rules will get you fired … if you violate them." The big man's face turned serious.

Max bobbed his head, listening.

"The first rule is we don't screw the company."

"Stands to reason."

"The second is we don't screw the help."

Max rolled his eyes. "Eh, that one's not as common. But, you know, I really had no intentions of—"

"It's not about you. I got that rule from an old friend of mine up in Georgia. He runs a nurse staffing agency or something like that. Lots of female employees around."

"Yeah, yeah, I can see where increased attention should be—"

"He said that nothing can disrupt a company more 'n having the help fraternizing and such and then bringing their problems into the workplace. Especially if the fraternizing is taking place between people in charge and people under their authority."

"Yeah, yeah, I can see that, too," Max agreed, swallowing hard.

"But I'm still just fooling with you, boy." John's eyes twinkled. "Hah! Besides, you don't stand a snowball's chance in hell with that lady anyway." He folded his arms and returned to watching after Nell—while Max watched him. A silent moment passed before John noticed.

"Yeah?" he asked.

"A question: you're really serious about the fraternizing part, aren't you, sir?" He thought he'd heard something more in the big man's voice.

John nodded. "Yeah, well, actually I am, son. Maybe. Do I look like I'm still dwelling on it or something?"

The accountant leaned close. "Another question: how'd you happen to hire Nell anyway? I mean, with all the men I've seen coming in this morning, and ... you don't let her stroll out back, do you? Through the storerooms? I mean, she's obviously quite well-endowed, and if you don't mind my saying, sir, she isn't too shy about showing it."

John took a deep breath. "Well, I'll have to agree with you there, son. She doesn't seem inclined toward modesty, does she? See, she'd been hired by Fleet, and late last year, after my old secretary announced that she wanted to leave and move to the

Panhandle—said she'd been getting threatening phone calls and thought this town wasn't safe anymore, you know?—anyway, Nell came to me and asked if she could move over to the position. My missus wasn't too happy with me about it, but, see, Nell said she'd become 'uncomfortable' working with Howard—and I'd had my suspicion already that he'd been trying to get something going. You know the rest, Max. I can hardly afford to lose Howard Fleet, and I certainly didn't want a bunch of legal stuff falling on me—I figured I could keep distance between the two of them."

"How'd Mr. Fleet like that?"

"Actually he was OK with the move. He said the change would be a good career move for Nell. And, you know, she seemed to like him just fine after the move—she wasn't bitter or anything. Neither was he. So, it was good all around—I guess."

"So you're OK with it all now? Something still bothering you?"

Walton sniffed. "Quite the perceptive auditor, Max. Actually, I was hoping for that. See, something does trouble me about the whole thing, about how things worked out so conveniently and all. And sometimes I catch her looking over at him, and ... well, it's probably nothing. With all what's going on with the company, its new product lines and growth, I guess I'm just getting a bit paranoid in my old age."

"But you'd like me to keep my eyes open when I'm out here? See if I notice anything?"

John smiled and nodded slightly. The stress lines at the corners of his eyes smoothed. "Yes, if you wouldn't mind. See, I'm not worried that anything is wrong with the books. I just don't want to think I was ... manipulated or something. Getting set up for something in the future. You know what I mean? I guess I'm more interested in your feelings, your observations about things when I'm not around."

"Yes, sir, I know what you mean. I'll keep my eyes open ... and I'll maybe take a closer look at duties—"

"I'm not saying that there's anything wrong with our finances, Max. You know that."

Caught in the in-betweens, aren't you? "John, I didn't say there was. I just have to check a lot of areas, and if you have certain misgivings … I won't say anything to anyone, John. And I'll keep you informed regardless. OK?"

Walton nodded and exhaled; he felt somewhat better. His wife had been after him, saying that things weren't "right" in the office between Howard and Nell. She'd said she could feel it "… but it's not that I worry about you and her, John." He smiled with the thought; his wife still called him her stud bull while he worried about his fading testosterone level.

"No, darlin', there's nothing to worry about with me," he'd assured her. Yet he had to admit to himself that the young woman's attentions weren't all that unwelcome. …

He noticed Max staring at him again, a question in his eyes. He realized he'd just been asked something—maybe about a desk? "Sorry, son. You caught me woolgathering or whatever that means. You're looking to get started, aren't you? Like I said, that'll be your office right there—next to the hallway back to payroll. The time clock's on the far side, and it shouldn't be too noisy here. I told you that already, didn't I?" He caught the other's slight nod. "All right then, tell you what: let's go on to the warehouse right now, and I'll introduce you to our manager, Rolando."

"Great!" Max stooped and picked up the bulging audit bag and the calculator case from off the floor alongside his feet where he'd dropped them and trudged over to the office, his rubber soles soundless on the floor. "Right here, huh? Say, this'll work fine." He noted the multiple electrical outlets lining the walls of the office. And a phone on the desk. "This is better than what I have at home." He deposited the calculator case on the desk and the audit bag on the floor and turned to rejoin Walton at the small office's door. He noticed a key in the door's inside knob and removed it, pulling the door shut behind. "OK if I lock up the space, John?" he asked.

Walton laughed; he was going to like this kid; he liked all people who were serious about their jobs. "You know, Max, ol' Tom didn't ask about locking this door last year, but I can see the need for it—for the security. You guys are supposed to be cautious with the records, aren't you? Tell you what: there's no telling how many people have keys to this door. So why don't you lock it for now, and tomorrow I'll have the locksmith in here? He'll give you the only keys to the door afterward—for your own use until you finish your work here. OK?" Without waiting for a reply, he struck off to his left, toward the double doors that dominated the back wall. Swinging them wide, he continued on, striding down the long glass-windowed corridor. "Come on, son," he called back over his shoulder. "Let me show you the place."

Max followed after, keeping an eye on John's broad back while surveying all around. *Place looks like a hospital. All white walls and plateglass windows.* He could see people on the other sides of the windows, working at various stations and machines in the expansive lab-like spaces.

"John!" he called. "Mr. Walton, what's this place over here and over there?"

Walton waited until he caught up. "This here is the development laboratory for our soft lenses on this side," he said, waving to his left, "and this side is for the cutting and shaping of our hard lenses. Minz didn't tell you about what all we do here, did he?"

The accountant pursed his lips, as if deciding on the answers available to him, and slowly shook his head.

John shook his head in return. "Dammit," he exclaimed mildly, "Randal does this to me every year. Ah well. Not in any hurry, are you? Got some time now?" Max nodded, and John proceeded with his mini-lecture, a well-practiced speech he'd given many times before—to new employees, to visiting scientists, to elementary-school classes, and, annually, to fresh-faced auditors. Also, of late, he'd given his discourse before several tours of investment bankers and prospective market makers. "For the future of VisualOptics," he'd said. Now, as they walked along, he talked without pause of lens-generator machines and multiple processes for scratch resistance and antireflection properties, of lasers and hard plastic lenses, of a kind of soft plasma lens now in development in the labs, and so on.

And on. Max felt his mouth drying and panic rising. There was no way in this world he was going to remember all this! *Now John's looking at me like I'm supposed to answer or something.* The man had halted outside another wide window, this one opening into a large bright room filled with more complex-looking machines and white-coated technicians working at the machines' consoles.

"Max?" Walton spoke again. "I asked if you remember what I said to you about lens blanks—I believe Randal calls them slugs." He pointed at a machine in the white expanse off to his right. "See those discs over there on the generator machine? ... which probably look like petri dishes to you?"

The accountant pressed close to the window to follow the guiding finger. "On that thing there?" he asked.

John snorted. "Yeah, on that 'thing there.' See, those blanks have certain curves and thicknesses and are stored in the warehouse ahead of us. When the prescriptions come in, we locate the appropriate blanks and transport them to this location in those trays and then cut and shape the lens as ordered; the scrip stays with the glass. And if frames are ordered—that's in another part of the warehouse—we group the lenses with the ordered frames. It's all rather structured and well coordinated. We sculpt hundreds and hundreds of lenses every day. And hard contacts. And, now, soft contacts. All to help people see better." He sounded quite proud of his company.

Max removed his own thick spectacles to examine them, flipping them back and forth. "Wow! I don't know if I'd ever thought about how these were made ... but I'd never have thought they'd started out looking like the bottoms of Coke bottles. Impressive."

John took the eyeglasses from Max's hands and held them above his head, examining them in the fluorescent lighting. "Plastic. Japanese. About a buck a slug, as Randal would say. You know I made him a pair about a month ago. Reading glasses."

"I've seen him with them," Max said. "Reading glasses." His boss wore his old-fashioned half-glasses at the end of his nose, peering over them while lecturing to clients and disciplining subordinates, enjoying the image he believed he projected: the hawkeyed, no-nonsense super CPA. "And Randal just paid a couple bucks for them?"

John snickered. "No, no, no. He wanted the clarity of the Swedish glass—about ten bucks a blank. I changed him about fifty dollars for the pair—including labor. And that's a deal. Hey, walk back here with me. Let me show you the storerooms."

He guided Max by his arm toward the stainless-steel double doors at the end of the corridor, about twenty yards away. Pushing in both doors and holding them wide, he dramatically turned back, his arms still outstretched, the enormous cathedral of a warehouse telescoping behind him. He was obviously very proud of the room's vastness, its amazing scale. "So what do you think?" he asked, anticipating the awed response usually elicited from impressed visitors."

The auditor said nothing.

"Max?" Walton prompted.

"Um, sir, you still have my glasses. You're a blur from where I stand."

"Oh yeah. Here. Your glasses. Now stand here. What do you think?"

Max whistled. "Big. And fuzzy. You know you got your fingers all over my lenses?"

John shook his head. It was going to be hard to impress this young fellow.

After Max had cleaned his eyeglasses with the front of his undershirt and his hot, moist breath, he ventured past John and farther into the open expanse that appeared to be filled, front to back, with freestanding racks of drawers—tall metal shelves of narrow boxes. He leaned left and gazed down the aisle between the blocks of racks, estimating that there were maybe fifty fluorescent-lit rows to the far wall, to the water fountain there. He straightened and counted ten blocks of racks across the width of the warehouse, noting that each double-sided rack contained twelve rows of drawers in height and perhaps fifty columns in width. Randomly selecting a drawer at head height, he carefully slid it open to its full reach—about thirty-six inches, he estimated—and discovered that the drawer was stuffed with paper envelopes, each containing a lens blank exactly like those he'd seen on the generator machine inside the lab. He lifted the first envelope in the row, carefully slid the glass disc from its protecting paper, and held it up to the overhead lights. It was heavier than he'd expected. "Not plastic," he noted.

John took the paper cover from him and read the code printed on the front. "Glass. Japanese. This one cost me about a buck—maybe a buck fifty—I'd have to check the curvature. Anyway, this is part of what you'll be counting—these drawers of blanks. This is the glass inventory here; plastic blanks are over there," he said, pointing, "through those double doors, in the next warehouse."

Now the young auditor was truly impressed; he whistled a long note that carried far into the cavernous space. A man walking across the long aisle ahead stopped, turned, looked back their way, and waved after ascertaining the source of the sound. John waved in return, and the man resumed his task: the annual counting of the inventory.

"Whew!" Max puffed, his breathing heavy, as if he'd been running. "Mr. Walton, it'll take a month to count all these lenses!"

John snorted. "Well, I guess I know why Randal doesn't tell you guys anything before he sends you out here. Otherwise you might not come. Hah!" He lightly patted the accountant's shoulder. "Tell you what, before you commit suicide, let me introduce you to Rolando here," he half turned to a man now standing at his side, "and then you can plan on how you want to do your auditing business. Attesting, isn't it? That what you call it?"

Max dumbly nodded; he hadn't noticed when the dark Latin-looking fellow had joined them.

Rolando nodded in return, saying, "Señor, welcome. Gracias. Maybe come avec Rolando ... eh ... to count."

Max's face fell. *The dude can hardly speak English. Two months! This inventory is gonna take two months to count!*

Still smiling, John shook his head. "Our droopily mustached friend here is enjoying you, Max. He's putting you on. He was born in Clearwater, got his engineering degree about two years ago from the University of Florida, and hasn't been south of Bradenton ... as far as I know. Probably never left the state. And if you took a language course in high school, your Spanish is probably better than his." He chuckled. "Sometimes I have to interpret for him with the men. And that's not saying much."

"But my French is better," Rolando brightly declared, extending his hand. "And we count using yardsticks around here, amigo." He'd seen the panic in the young auditor's face. "See? So many envelopes per yard ... just multiply. See? Quick." He resisted adding, "Trust me."

Max shook the man's hand. He was feeling somewhat better, slightly mollified. *Maybe only one month then.*

• • •

Eight hours later, he was again shaking the manager's hand. "I cannot believe your men counted all this stuff, all these drawers in all these storehouses." He took the copies of the count sheets Rolando held out to him. "I mean," he continued, "that was a lot of work those guys did."

The dark man smiled broadly, flashing bright, white teeth. "Aw, they do it all the time. With as much glass as we move through here, we've got to know what we've got in stock." He raised his hand and rubbed his thumb and middle finger together. "It's our profit-sharing thing, señor."

Max copied the gesture, finger rubbing thumb. "So, with John and Howard taking the company public, are your guys going to be even better off?"

Rolando's facial expression hardened, and his coloration deepened a shade; he dropped his raised hand. "Mr. Fleet is not as open to the men as John is. We're not sure how this whole thing is going to work out." A silent second passed, and the bright smile returned. "Hey, forget what I said. OK? Yeah, we'll do OK. So, see you tomorrow, amigo? Maybe eat some lunch with us tomorrow?"

Max was puzzled by the man's sudden change in attitude. *There's more to this.* He decided he would definitely have lunch with this guy one day during the week. "Yeah, thanks. I was worried you guys didn't eat lunch or something—I'm starved. And I'll be here for a while, I guess. Randal Minz, my boss, is coming out later to assist me. He said he'd be by today but didn't make it."

Rolando huffed with the mention of the name. "Randal is coming this week? Great! That sucker stuck me with the lunch tab last year. Invited me out and—it's about his turn to buy."

• • •

The next morning, Max again arrived early, this time parking his Chevy farther out in the employees' lot, placing the defaced side of his vehicle toward the encircling fence. *Embarrassing.* After edging his way out on the driver's side, he opened the rear door and leaned in, retrieving his audit bag and his calculator case from off the seat. "Sharp ride you got there, Americano CPA," he muttered to himself. *But until Randal gets around to paying bonuses—*

Something poked him in the small of his back, abruptly terminating his thoughts; he turned with a start. *Rolando!* "Whew! Dang! You scared the crap outta me."

"Oh, sorry, dude," the man apologized; he didn't smile with the moment. "Sorry, man. Hey, listen, just in case you take stuff personally: after you left last night, Fleet came around and told us that we are not to be talking with you. He said it could mean our jobs if we're seen talking with you. He said he's the only one authorized by the board to interface with you and that's the way it's meant to be: all information requests are to come through him. So, if you wouldn't mind—"

"Was it the same last year?" Max questioned. "Was that the way it was … during last year's audit?" He was still breathing deep from having been surprised.

Rolando stepped back and angled his head, thinking. "Just at the last, I guess," he said. "Apparently someone said something to Tom—you know, the auditor last year?—something that Fleet had wanted to be kept in-house, and I guess he got pretty hot about it. So, anyway, now you know … but tell Randal that he still owes me a lunch. OK? But just not around here. OK?"

"Yeah, OK. I'll tell him."

"By the way," Rolando continued, now scanning the parking lot to the front, "if you've got an extra twenty on you, some of these Mexican dudes' kids will compound out those scratches on the side of your ride there, man. Bet you're thinking it looks like shit, aren't you? You must have really ticked off somebody."

"Twenty dollars?"

"Yeah."

"Today."

"Yeah … but I'm telling you that there ain't nothing can be done for those gouges down to bare metal. But the kids will color over those with a marker so they'll be less noticeable. OK?"

"Done," Max agreed. He fumbled in his wallet for the single twenty-dollar bill he had there. *Good thing I brought a PB&J for lunch.* He handed over the bill.

Rolando absently palmed it without looking down, his eyes still roaming over the roofs of the parked cars. "OK, dude. I'll pass it on. No one will come to tell you about it; it'll just be done by tonight. And I'll tell you thanks right now. Some of these guys work two jobs and appreciate any chance for some additional bread."

"OK. I appreciate it, too, since it'd be a while before I could get to it. Times are tough. Hey, can you help me with this calculator case here?"

Rolando grimaced. "Sorry, man. No can do. Fleet might come driving up … and the man don't joke around. Understand? Maybe we'll see each other later on. OK?" He turned without waiting for an answer and trotted away, heading to the shadows at the far side of the lot, where he would walk around the building to the rear entrance, the warehouse.

Wasn't kidding. Max watched after the furtive man until he'd disappeared behind cars parked a dozen rows over. *Strange.* He picked up his two cases and trudged off, ambling toward the front entrance's glass doors that now reflected the rising sun, rethinking Rolando's words as he walked. *Don't talk to the auditors, huh?* He scuffed his shoes along in the loose gravel. *Damn!*

Once inside the building and entering his assigned office space, he dropped his audit bag to the carpet and hoisted the calculator case to the desk for unpacking. As he plugged in the machine, he heard a tap at the door and looked up. "Mr. Walton—John," he greeted. "Good morning, sir."

The CEO stepped inside and tossed over a set of wire-ringed keys, as Max straightened. "Keys," he simply stated. "The only keys," he added, and then he was gone.

"Um ..." Max had considered asking about Fleet's directive. *Too late—he's gone. Well, anyway, maybe I can leave more stuff here at night now?* He dangled the keys on the ring, briefly examining them before slipping them into his pants pocket. *That'll be nice, I guess.* Flipping the switch on the back of the calculator, he listened to it cycle to life as he circled the desk. Seating himself, he rolled over to straddle the tall audit case and began the process of unloading his papers and files for the day.

The first files he pulled from the case were the audit programs, the work guides detailing the steps the auditors were to consider, and the documentation they were to accumulate during the course of the audit of their client's books and records. *Forming a reasonable basis for opinion.* He lined up the files on the desk: his audit program and the prior year's audit program—the one completed by Tom. His virgin file was scarcely a tenth the thickness of Tom's. He sighed. *Gonna be a long couple of weeks.* Another tap at the door interrupted his thoughts: *John's assistant, Nell!* She stood smiling at him from the doorway, her teeth sparkling, her dress tight and very short, her heels high, and her hands folded and held slightly below her ample …

Max forced his gaze upward, to perhaps consider a spot on the ceiling, slightly above the woman's flowing blond tresses. "Hey … eh, hey," he greeted, momentarily unable to rise to his feet. "Good morning … Nell. What … what can I do for you?" *Please, Lord. Make it personal.*

She flashed another dazzling smile. "Max," she began, saying his name as if it were two syllables, high to low in tone. "Mr. Fleet said to give you these." She bent low, placing several packets of papers onto the chair beside the door. "Internal financial statements and schedules, some other accounting stuff—something to get you started, he said." She turned as if to leave and then turned back, lingering in the doorway. "Say, did John already give you a key to this office this morning? Maybe two keys—both the keys to this office?" She edged back into the office. "See, he'd called the locksmith yesterday to rekey this lock," she said, caressing the silver doorknob like it was a living thing, "and, this morning, the man came and left before I arrived and just now dropped off the invoice. So we were thinking that perhaps John gave you both keys when he should have only given you one. See?" she added brightly. "One for the janitor?"

The wide-eyed accountant was already digging into the depths of his pockets, searching for the ring. *Maybe she'd like my car keys, my house keys, my loose change, to bear my firstborn.* His glasses were still fogged from having watched her deposit the papers on the chair.

"The invoice," she said, "that the locksmith left with Mr. Fleet charged for two keys, so, naturally, we were wondering if—"

Max didn't hear the remainder of Nell's sentence; his internal alarm sounded. "Mr. Fleet"? "We were wondering"? Something was wrong here; he'd need to be careful.

"Eh, Nell, wouldn't John have left a key with you to give to the janitorial folks … if he'd wanted them to have it? Or is it possible that John kept a key—you said the invoice noted that two keys were made? Do you have the invoice with you?" He held out his hand.

Nell's eyes narrowed, and her smile faded as she studied the seated man and his raised hand. She was not used to males dithering when she'd expressed a need—her need. And she was not certain that the invoice she'd carried to Howard had actually detailed the making of two keys. And perhaps she should not have mentioned that she'd been dispatched by Fleet. She relit her smile and twisted her way into the room, over to the side of the desk. She leaned forward, palms flat to the desktop, and tightened her shoulders—accentuating cleavage. She watched Max's eyes. "Oh, I said Mr. Fleet? I meant Mr. Walton. Mr. Walton seems to have remembered giving you both keys, and, you know, the maintenance department will need access in here—to clean after hours. You know?" She almost batted her perfect eyelashes and pursed her full lips.

Max felt the blood rush to his face; he'd never ever before received such a look from a beautiful woman—or any woman, for that matter. *Like in the movies!* At that moment, he definitely knew something was wrong: things like this didn't happen to him. He exhaled loudly and dropped his eyes to his workpapers. "Um, Nell," he stammered, "maybe there's been some miscommunication or something. See, I've only got the one key." He'd stopped digging in his pocket. "Maybe John took the extra key to the maintenance department himself. You really should go ask him." He avoided looking up because he feared she was now glaring down at him. And she was.

Nell's amazingly perfect teeth were now hidden behind tight lips. She abruptly turned and stamped from the tiny office, clicking her way back across the terrazzo floor, leaving Max alone to puzzle out the meaning of this encounter—along with the one with

Rolando. *Trust?* Even though he was a neophyte auditor, he sensed that this was not going to be a normal engagement by any measure.

• • •

When lunchtime arrived, he was still mulling over the events as he sorted through the schedules. Max knew that Nell worked for John, yet she'd been sent by Fleet. He'd seen the uncertainty in her eyes when he'd requested to see the invoice, and he was concerned by the young woman's pressuring response to his reluctance. *Something's up. And we both know it. Access in here—to my stuff? Keeping tabs on me? Don't talk to the auditor?* He'd have to be careful—careful in what he recorded on paper and what he said aloud. He'd call Randal tonight—from home. *I wonder what Tom did last year.*

His stomach rumbled. *Lunch!* He'd brought his lunch from home today. Yesterday, he hadn't eaten.

Fitting his still-thin audit program back into the audit bag and thumbing shut its rolling combination locks, he swiveled around to the credenza and slid out its various drawers, searching for a suitable place to deposit (hide) certain work papers and correspondence for the short periods when he'd be away from his desk. Even with its latches engaged and its locks' numbers scrambled, the audit case was hardly a secure repository for confidential documents; it could be easily opened with a bent paper clip (Lou had shown Max the technique when the fledgling accountant had first been issued the case—and had immediately forgotten its combination).

Behind! He discovered that, below one of the fully extended drawers, there was about six inches of free space. He could store confidential files and programs under those two drawers if he had to, whenever he was to be away from his desk for any length of time. *Dang!* He then realized that he'd still have to lug a fully packed audit bag to and from his car each day; he couldn't risk leaving sensitive documents hidden in the office for the night. *Too much time.* "Well, then that'll be just what I have to do," he vowed to the empty air as he stood, brown bag in hand. "And maybe I'll see Rolando in the employees' lunchroom? Yeah!" He wanted to talk more with the storeroom manager about Fleet's directives and about Howard and Nell's relationship—about whom she really worked for. *And maybe about other observations and any general employee concerns. He'd know what's happening.*

He re-spun the locks on the case and, on a whim, laid a single ultrafine Pentel lead across the top of its folded flaps. *Probably just being excessively paranoid … per McVeigh.* Last year, the professor had told his auditing class several "war stories" from his days in public practice. One story, Max now remembered, was about the time Gene had trapped a dishonest clerk by similarly marking his desk drawers and exposing her clandestine and forced entries into his confidential space … and his Hershey's bars. The class had laughed heartily at the story, and the professor had made his point: he had recounted the incident, he'd said, to balance out their textbook's serious and frequent admonishments to "stay aware," "maintain an independent mind-set," and "trust but confirm." He'd said that, in reality, the practice of auditing was more of an endurance test than a glamourous, crime-seeking endeavor—a pursuit that constantly weighed practical costs (including potential litigation fees) with third-party information needs. He'd added that any auditor—especially one who'd go on to write textbooks—should expect the major portion of his or her worktime to consist of mental adventures, not physical ones.

"So maintain your perspective, and keep it cost effective," Gene had said. "You're not double oh seven."

Just the same … Max looked about the room one more time, attempting to memorize objects and their placement. He noted with satisfaction that when he stood fully erect, the graphite lead on the top of his audit case was all but invisible. *So let's go eat.* He locked the office door behind, using one of the wire-ringed keys, and strode across the lobby and through the double doors leading to the laboratories and the warehouses; the lunchroom was off to the right in the hallway. John had pointed out its sign yesterday, saying, "You'll probably want to chow down in there with everybody else. The ice tea's free … and I know you're an accountant. Hah!" He'd snorted, rapped Max on the shoulder, and then walked away—without telling him the joke's punch line. *Nothing funny about tea … and it's free!*

Standing outside the lunchroom door, his hand on the knob, he could hear loud voices and laughter coming from the inside. *Great!* He was looking forward to seeing Rolando again. He twisted the doorknob and peeked through the widening opening; the place was full—and noisy. VisualOptics' employees looked to be really enjoying their lunches and their friends. *Yeah!* He walked in. *Should be fun.*

Then heads turned, and conversations faded. After noting his entrance, the gathered personnel immediately ceased their banter and dropped their attentions to the tabletops and their respective meals. Silence reigned.

"Whoa," he breathed. *Ever feel like a turd in a punch bowl?* "Eh, hello," he ventured in general greeting, and then loudly cleared his throat. "Hey, everybody," he tried again, adding a tentative finger wave. *Maybe they think I'm a new manager or something? Maybe taking names?* "Anybody?" Two people looked up and offered wane smiles and brief, courteous nods before returning to their lunches. *At least I know I exist. Where's Rolando?* He didn't see the man, but he remembered his words from earlier today: "… it could mean our jobs if we're seen talking with you." *Aww, man!*

He scanned the group again, looking for the manager's dark face. *Not here.* He'd have to ask about him. *Later,* he decided; he was starved.

Selecting a vacant chair at the closest table, Max strolled over and tossed his brown bag onto the open space across from an older woman munching away on her potato chips piled high on a napkin, and beside the bearded guy draining the last of the contents of his tall paper cup. *Tea!* That reminded him. He looked about the room, searching for the free tea dispenser and seeing a pair of shiny urns on the far counter, there beside the sink. Leaving his lunch on the table, he ambled over to the first urn and leaned down to read its label. "Sweet tea," he murmured aloud. "That's great." He lifted two Dixie cups from the stacks between the urns, filled both cups to the brim, and turned to retrace his steps to his lunch bag. *Gosh!* Except for his battered brown sack, the table was now bare; the woman and the bearded guy had finished their meals and were leaving the room, softly closing the door behind. *Click.* The silence remained. *Didn't even hear them sliding their seats back.*

He walked on to the table, set down his cups, and seated himself. *Plenty of room, I guess. But still very uncomfortable.* As he unfolded his paper sack and spread his napkin, he looked left and right, trying to make eye contact with anyone who'd flick a glance his way. *Anyone? Anyone?* He dumped his sandwich from his bag onto the napkin. *Whump!* No one turned with the sound; his fellow diners seemed content to either stare vacantly off into space or to continue to closely analyze the molecular makeup of their own plastic-wrapped repasts. No eyes were to stray in his direction. *So just eat your lunch and go ... and call Randal tonight.* "And maybe I should drop by John Walton's office to ask what's going on here," he stage-whispered. Still, no one peeked, and no one replied. His embarrassment had turned to irritation. "I think I just might," he declared.

Well, Max, he thought, *if you choose to do that, what'll you do if John tells you that Fleet was right to restrict unnecessary communications between you and the employees? And if he tells you to pull up your big-boy shorts and get on with the job?* After all, he wasn't being paid to be the employees' friend, was he? Yet while he felt the CEO would empathize with him and probably appreciate hearing about this treatment, the information would still be secondhand ... and Mr. Fleet was a much-valued employee. John had stated several times his belief that the man was a key link to VisualOptics' future. So if he went to Walton now and recited Rolando's words, he'd actually be putting the CEO in a bad position—to say nothing of himself and Randal—and Rolando. And what did he expect the man to do? *Fire his CFO? Based on what? My discomfort?* He couldn't do that; he couldn't say that. *Fleet's actions might, in fact, be the very defensive actions any professional financial executive would employ ... especially if his company was going public and he wanted to control information releases to the public. After all, such info is a really big deal.* "Financial statements present fairly ..." He'd spoken aloud in his ruminations; his voice trailed off; he looked around the room: all the other tables were now mostly bare; the few remaining diners were standing, and chairs were being pushed in. Still no one glanced his way. *But they're the ones looking embarrassed.* He watched them leave.

The door closed behind the last employee. "So ol' Elvis done left the building," he loudly observed in a broad Appalachian accent, since he now addressed only vacant chairs and a barely touched sandwich. "And Max, ol' boy, ol' John won't want to listen to you and your speculations neither. 'Specially if it's like the ol' boy who cries wolf too often. In fact, you just might want to wait before talking to Randal tonight, too." He knew his boss's interests tended to the practical—the progress of the audit—that and its accumulating costs. "So unless you see something that might affect that ol' opinion on the face of the financials, you'd better just keep your cogitations to yourself."

But would it help John to know his secretary might be more loyal to Fleet than to himself? "As smart as that guy is, I'd expect he already knows that. Hmm." He considered the value he placed on Walton's opinions—especially those about him personally ... and he'd only known the man for a few days. "Go figure," he whispered, shaking his head.

"So just keep your thoughts to yourself," he concluded, "for now. And don't go off half-cocked but be vigilant—as the textbooks say." He folded his lunch bag and slipped it into his back pocket as he got to his feet—*for tomorrow's lunch.* He'd choose times and places later. "That is, if I eat at all tomorrow." He'd hardly tasted his sandwich, the majority of which he now tossed in the garbage can, along with his sweet tea. "I should've asked where they kept the free ice when I had the chance."

Another thought came to him as he closed the door behind and headed toward the steel double doors: *Could Fleet have bugged the lunchroom?* He felt a momentary twinge of alarm. *Bet he'd think I'm crazy talking to myself like that. Or that I'm my own best entertainment—the truth.*

When he reached the tiny office in the front, he found a huge cardboard box blocking the doorway. He pushed at it with his foot. "Heavy." Kneeling on the terrazzo, he carefully lifted its lid. "Dang!" It was completely filled with wide sheets of green-screen computer paper. He lifted the top sheet; it appeared to be a printout of VisualOptics' general ledger. "Or at least that's what it says it is." The page was filled border to border with printed lines of letters and numbers, and, except for the title line and the date range, each line appeared to be random gibberish. "And I bet that's exactly what I asked for," he sighed. Prior to leaving for lunch, he'd tried to phone Nell with his information request and had left his message on her recorder. "Dang!" He puffed his cheeks in exasperation and pulled out the sides of the box, trying to see the pages farther down the pile. "All the same, top to bottom," he surmised. "Certainly not what I expected."

Yet the lines of data looked somewhat familiar. "Machine language?" he asked himself. "Programming?" During his tour of duty in the military, he'd monitored and repaired communications equipment—primarily teletype and its computer-like replacement, digital subscriber terminal equipment or DSTE—and learned to read the various codes used in text transmissions. He'd been proud of his ability to scan and quickly translate the data bits from punch cards and paper tape—faster than most operators, he'd claimed.

"At least it's not ASCII," he sniffed, leaning back on his haunches. "More than just holes in tape and zeros and ones—but it's still just a damn data dump." He'd requested access to a detailed general ledger for the entire fiscal year—*and that's exactly what this is*, he guessed, *but without formatting and spacing*. "The names are all here, and the numbers are all here, I bet—Fleet's little joke." It was now clear to him that the CFO intended to control this audit and to delve out financial data as he saw fit. "It's no wonder Tom quit."

Max got to his feet and glanced about, searching for spectators to his frustration. He'd halfway expected to see Fleet or Nell standing in their respective office doorways, watching him from far across the wide lobby and smirking. *Making me feel stupid.* But he appeared to be alone in the room; the solid doors across the way remained closed.

Digging deep in his pocket, he extracted the wire-ringed set of keys. He selected one and inserted it into the door's lock; the freshly oiled mechanism turned easily, and the latch assembly clicked open; the door swung inward. He stepped through the widening gap and turned back to drag the cardboard box on through the doorway; he aligned it with his audit case behind the desk, being careful not to bump the latter's tall leather sides. Next, moving over to the case, he examined its folded top panels and noted the position of the planted Pentel lead: it was exactly where he'd left it. He puffed a scornful laugh and shook his head. "Paranoid, Max, paranoid," he muttered. "That's just what you are." *But just in case ...* He again reconnoitered the high-ceilinged lobby through the open doorway. "Nope," he determined. "Still nobody watching me from way over there."

He eased himself onto the chair behind the desk. *Now if I can just concentrate for the remainder of the afternoon ...*

• • •

A knock sounded at his door, and he looked up. John Walton was standing in the opening, his coat draped across his arm. "Time to wrap it up, son," he announced. "The day's done."

"Geez, Mr. Walton, what time is it anyway?" Max yawned and stretched, angling his head to peer out the office door, past the man and toward the front windows: it appeared to still be daylight outside. *But faded.*

"John," corrected the CEO. "Just John. Remember? And it is incredible, isn't it? Time kind of gets away from a man when he's engaged in something and really concentrating; hours go by like nothing. And I can tell that you like your job ... and you're obviously very good at it; you don't even know you're hours past quitting time. Now, with me, my bladder would be telling me the time—in minutes and seconds."

Max nodded in agreement; suddenly he too felt the urgent need to visit the facilities. "Um, pardon me, sir!" He lunged to his feet.

Walton leaned to one side, allowing the young man to scurry by.

Ten minutes later, he locked the entrance door behind them. "Close call?" John teased; Max grinned in reply. "By the way," he continued, "I surely didn't mean to rush you in there; you might've had some questions for me or something. And you know, son, you could've stayed on if you'd wanted to; you had the place all to yourself. Just the nighttime might be a bit lonely ... and there *are* the ghosts ..."

"Nearsighted auditor ghosts, I bet. Hah! Naw, I should've been watching the clock more closely. And questions? I'll try and hold 'em until Randal's here ... Friday, I think. I didn't want to bother you or anything."

"You sound like Fleet," John groused. "That guy is continually worrying about me ... being bothered by questions and people coming in to see me. Max, I want to be asked! ... to hear people's questions and to make decisions! That's one of ways I know what's going on. See? I don't ever want to work in an ivory tower, holding myself above it all while I await only the infrequent questions and esoteric inquiries." He huffed and shook his head. "*Esoteric*—that's Howard's word."

"Well, then OK ... sir. Does Mr. Fleet, eh, think you'll get spread too thin to focus on the really important stuff or something?"

John huffed through his nose again. "More likely he wants to do what I do—no, no, I shouldn't say that. Not to the auditor anyway, hah!" It was a brittle laugh. "Forget I said that. I'm tired. I'm ..."

Max nodded, walking alongside the man, saying nothing. *Maybe now I should ask about—*

"See," John resumed, "when you've worked for years ... shoulder to shoulder with the engineers, the sales guys, the craftsmen, the—the clerks and janitors, well, the practice of being in the thick of things is hard to break. Why, I used to bring in a keg of beer and Cokes on Fridays and cook hot dogs and such to get together to hear about the staff and their families ... but we don't do that anymore. With growth comes separateness and union organizing and executives wanting turf and decision-making authority and ... change!" He was shaking his bowed head again; his face was drawn and serious.

"Yeah," Max replied, "I can understand that. But I guess that means you're successful, too, huh? And I guess if you're growing, you're going to spill water if you try to do everything. You have to delegate at some point." *As if I'd know. I sound like Pollyanna.*

"Well, son, you're not telling me anything I don't already know ... and I've tried to do that all along. I guess I wasn't being clear with you: I don't want to *make* all the decisions; I just want to be kept informed of the decisions. Those engineers, those scientists, those guys stocking the warehouses—they make the decisions. They've got the smarts and experience to run their own areas. They'd make better decisions than me any day—I know that. And I know enough about managing to encourage them to make those decisions. It makes the job interesting for them. And I know enough to back them up when they do make those decisions. But, see ... you know, I really don't need to be talking like this with you. I hardly know you from beans, but I know that—I feel that—you're good at your job, you're intimate with my company—or will be anyway—and, heck, if you can't talk to the auditors, whom can you talk to? Hah! The auditors gotta be discreet. Isn't that what they teach you?"

Max gave the older man a sharp look—and then smiled. He hadn't a clue how big-company CEOs were supposed to act, but he definitely liked this guy. *Trusted him.* "You know, I have had something on my mind ... about an order given and that certain people ..." His voice trailed off as he arranged his thoughts. *What could John say about Fleet's directive concerning auditor contacts? Would he then confront the man? And would Howard retaliate against me? And maybe John is OK with Nell still answering to Fleet?* He again decided he'd maybe better wait and talk with Randal before baring his soul and thoughts to Mr. Walton. "Umm ... sir ... John, the office keys you gave me: did you mean to give me both keys? Does Nell—or maintenance—need the second key?"

John returned the questioning look. "I thought you guys were required to safeguard your auditing programs and supersecret manuals. That not right?" He paused for a second and then winked and patted Max on his back. "So I called the locksmith myself and had him rekey the door right before you arrived ... and gave you both keys. You could have left that thing locked up in the office, you know." He glanced down as they walked, at the heavy audit bag Max carried by his side. "Or you just might want the exercise, huh? Anyway, you *are* planning on giving them back before you leave, aren't you? The keys, I mean? And you *can* dump your own trash, can't you?" He laughed. "You know, now that I think about it, I believe ol' Tom used to take his garbage home with him."

"Of course I can. But your secretary said ... never mind. Thanks." He'd wait. "Yeah, Randal will be here Friday, and maybe I'll have more questions for you then. OK?"

"Sure. Whenever. So may I wish you a fine and pleasant evening for now? See you bright and early tomorrow?" The CEO raised his hand for a quick wave as he angled off to the left, striding toward the late-model car parked at the front of the vast gravel-rocked lot. "I expect that's your Chevy sitting way over there," he called back, pointing toward the fence.

"Yes, that's my car. Good night, sir—John." *I wonder if the marks on my doors mostly came out.*

"By the way," John yelled again over his shoulder, "I think the boys did a pretty good job on your door and quarter panel. They worked pretty hard on those bare-metal places." He waved again and marched on, without further comment or inquiry as to the cause.

• • •

The new morning came, and Max again chose to park his car close by the fence. As he made his way toward the distant front entrance, shifting his heavy audit bag from hand to hand as he crunched along (he'd left his calculator case in the tiny office the night before), he scanned over the rooftops of the parked vehicles, hoping for a glimpse of Rolando's brown droopily mustached visage. *Not here.* He supposed the man was closely adhering to Fleet's directive. *Probably a smart thing for him to do.* So he turned his thoughts to his goal for the day: *transaction tests.*

Yesterday, at various times throughout the afternoon, Nell had shown up outside his office door, tapping on the metal jamb with her brightly polished nails, to deliver copies of analysis schedules that "Mr. Fleet said you'd be needing … sooner or later." When he had first asked about what the reports covered, she'd raised her eyebrows and shrugged as if to say … he wasn't quite sure what she was trying to say; she'd not actually chosen to reply. Instead, after unceremoniously dumping the materials on the corner of his desk, she'd simply wheeled about on her tall heels and ticked her way back across to their offices. But Max was relatively certain that her thoughts were not complimentary ones. *Especially after the way she stormed out of here about the extra-key thing.* Thus, up until the time Mr. Walton had roused him last evening, he'd spent the major portion of his afternoon reviewing and indexing the mounds of PBC ("prepared by client") schedules and not working on his planned tests of transactions. *So I'll start with that today. There's time.* Tomorrow—Thursday—he'd concentrate on the balance sheet, and on Friday, while Randal was here, he'd track the selected transaction information back to source documentation—bank statements, invoices, time cards—*whatever they've got. And I'll talk to Randal about Fleet's directive ... and about Mr. Walton's ramblings yesterday.* He'd figured that, at some prior time, the CEO had also talked to his boss, or to Tom, in a like fashion. *So maybe it means something ... or nothing.*

Stepping onto the sidewalk at the building's entrance, he stamped his feet several times, trying to remove some of the accumulated dust from his shoes. Another fifteen steps, and he was standing before the tiny office's door, selecting one of the identical keys on the wire ring and then fitting it in the lock. *Scratches!* Max noticed possibly new gleaming threads on the knob's aluminum surface. *Whoa!* He straightened and searched about, making sure he was not being observed—*while looking stupid.* Then he bent low to more closely examine the metal around the keyhole. *Yes!* The scratches were freshly glinting, as if someone had recently tried to pick the lock. *Maybe during the overnight hours. Now why would someone do that?* His next fear was that the lock had been re-keyed—but his key slid smoothly into the slot and turned easily in the cylinder. *So then maybe someone had another key made?* He'd have to give that more study. *Regardless of the reason,* he sighed with the thought, *I'm still gonna be shuttling this friggin' audit case back and forth.* And hiding his workpapers under drawers whenever he left the office during the day.

He pushed open the door and eased his way around the desk to the chair. He sat heavily and leaned forward, clicking open the audit bag he'd dropped at his feet and then pivoting around to face the credenza and his stacked PBC papers. *Wait! Listen.* He spun back toward the desk, having heard the faint heel-toe rhythm of leather-soled shoes crossing the reception area. *Fleet!* He stood and watched the doorway, thinking that the CFO had not bothered himself to cross the lobby to talk with him since his arrival—since their restaurant meeting.

"Good morning, Howard," he cheerfully greeted, when the tall well-tailored man appeared in the opening. *And wearing his jacket, too,* Max noted, supposing the chief financial officer to be the only man on the premises to be actually wearing a suit coat. *Even John carries his jacket in and out the building. Too hot outside.*

"Yes, umm ... Max," Fleet replied, after the practiced pause: his way of making sure the insignificant auditor understood how diffi-cult it was for him to remember an insignificant name. "Good morn-ing, Max," he said again, stepping forward to place the tall stack he carried onto the corner of the desk: envelopes that immediately tipped and slid across the desktop's surface.

"Good morning, Howard," Max repeated. He could see the envelopes were stamped and addressed. "And these are ...?"

"These are your confirmations for this fiscal year, Max. Since we've closed some accounts at Rutland Bank, I did not attempt to repeat all the prior year's confirmations. I have also included account confirmations for our ten largest suppliers and our ten larg-est-balance customers—they do not wish to correspond directly with you." He managed a tight, condescending smile and turned to leave. "OK. Nothing else then?" he questioned over his shoulder, although it sounded more like a statement.

"Legal-rep letters, sir?" Max called.

"Pardon?" The tall man stopped and rotated about on his expensive leather heels. His face suggested he'd not expected a reply. "Did you say something ... Max?"

"Howard, I'll have to talk with Randal about the prior year's practices, but I sincerely doubt that you, the audit client, will be permitted to select the outside parties with whom we wish to com-municate in confirming balance sheet amounts and transactions. I mean, that *is* where our independence comes in, I think. I was ... eh ... joking when I asked about legal letters, but the lawyers and investment bankers—"

"I do not joke, and you will not be allowed to directly con-tact our investment bankers," Fleet boomed, "or our attorneys.

Furthermore, your correspondence with any attorney will come only through me. Me only. Understood?"—another question voiced like a statement.

Max considered the CFO's glaring orbs through equally unwavering eyes. After several more long uncomfortable seconds passed, he nodded his acknowledgment ... that he had heard the man's commands—but only that he'd heard what had been said. He vowed he would talk with Randal before he said anything more. *Maybe this is why Tom left?*

"Good," Fleet curtly replied and again turned away, returning to his offices across the wide lobby with measured, unwavering strides.

The young auditor listened to the fading footfalls until carpet was reached. Then he listened to the blood pulse in his ears. *Breathe, Max, just breathe,* he instructed himself, hoping his rage had not been apparent in his face. *Sit down. Good. Now breathe. Breathe.* He had not wanted to give Fleet any satisfaction in knowing he'd been so easily angered. "It's just business," he repeated in a whisper. "Just business. Nothing personal."

But it was, he knew. It was very personal with him—as was almost everything he did in business or elsewhere—or else he didn't do it. He'd had several friends tell him that, in business-related settings, they'd learned to mentally situate themselves outside of any personal involvements in the ongoing proceedings, to watch and react much like they were part of an audience rather than participants. *Cool. Breathe. Control.* But, to him, that sounded as if they'd merely learned to mute everything—or else stopped caring altogether.

He had difficulty imagining a world where people simply acted out their parts, spending the major part of their days interacting in play situations, receiving their proverbial paychecks and then leaving their workdays behind, going out in the world to engage their passions in other, truer-for-them realities. *Or not—because how's that possible anyway? To find satisfaction in a life where the major part of the day's events and happenings are all impersonal?* "That would surely make for a very long and very dull existence," he concluded, leaning forward on the desk, "to say nothing of the squandered gobs of precious time."

But maybe it's just our terminology that's different? he now reasoned. "Hot, instinctive reaction versus reasoned, thought-out response? Or maybe pervasive distrust and fear of confrontation … justifying deception? In other words, let's just play like it's impersonal," he muttered, his eyes hooded, his forehead resting on desk-propped fists, "and the winner … is the one … who's the best actor. Yeah! Still sounds dull to me … and cowardly."

He exhaled again and slumped backward in the chair, his pondering complete. His anger had ebbed, and he could refocus on his work. *Maybe.* He reached down into his case and lifted the first file he touched: his audit program. He flipped through its pages and stopped on a new page; he'd made his decisions: First, he would devote the remainder of this day and the next in testing transactions. *No-brainer stuff,* he thought. Second and most importantly, on Friday, he would have a long, long discussion with Randal—and offer his resignation. He'd concluded that it was not possible for him to continue to perform the VisualOptics' audit. He'd have to find work elsewhere; he was not cut out for this. He would complete the ticking and tying tasks, but he would not—could not—continue to manage the engagement and interact effectively if Mr. Fleet continued to interfere, to dictate. He would tell Randal that, and while he did not hate the CFO … *but I do. I actually do hate the man,* he then realized. Howard Fleet was rude, obnoxious, overbearing, vain—every attribute he could imagine disliking in another person.

He's a plain mean SOB! Max didn't know where this last thought had originated; it was an inner feeling, a push of emotion more than an observation. *Yeah, a really mean bastard! A black soul! So … can you last until Friday?* He wondered now if he would be able to stay there, to work until the weekend. He had calmed himself, he'd thought, but he wasn't certain if he could continue to feign basic courtesies, to hide his very unprofessional feelings from anyone—including Fleet. "So ol' Randal had better find another auditor quick if he wants to keep the client—you should call him tonight … and then you should be looking for another job, boy." He listened to his words as he spoke them; he was at peace with the decision. "You've gotta always be willing to move on if it comes to that; there's a line to be crossed. Job's important but not that important."

• • •

The remainder of Wednesday had passed quickly; Mr. Fleet did not cross the wide lobby again that day.

That evening, Max called Randal at home three times and received a busy signal each time. He decided he'd try again early Thursday—maybe.

• • •

Now Thursday was speeding by.

Late in the afternoon, Max dialed Nell's extension and requested several more invoices, adding, "And perhaps access to the purchase journals?" Since yesterday—after having found a way to work with the massive general ledger report—he'd progressed quickly with the routine task of transaction selection, and his audit program had quickly fattened. He was ready now to test, to tick and tie, and he needed the purchase journals to do much of that.

At first, VisualOptics' detailed general ledger printout for the fiscal year, the two-foot-plus-high pile of green-screen paper that had been printed off in its entirety and deposited in his doorway, had stymied him. *Undecipherable,* he'd thought. *Even reading the tiny type is terrible.* However, recalling his data-processing days in the military, in the early seventies, when computer memory storage had been exceedingly expensive and programmers learned to be extremely efficient in their datum displays, he realized he'd seen similarly printed media. *Memory backups! And this is just another memory dump—only without spaces.*

"But, you know, it's probably all there, and it's probably exactly what I'd asked for," he had told himself. "And that asshole Fleet's had some great fun with me." Then he had set to work, searching for whatever information he could glean from the huge volume … and eventually he discovered it—the logic—the key. After an hour or so of thumbing through pages, he'd identified certain constants in the lines of numbers that opened the GL's numbers to him. Using his ruler and colored pencils, he'd mapped out account numbers, source journals, dates, descriptions, amounts—almost everything an auditor needed to sample transactions. *But I'll probably still need some confirmation of my assumptions,* he'd thought.

So, this morning, after having managed to put aside his wounded feelings from the prior day, he'd padded across the terrazzo seeking Mr. Fleet's attention.

The meeting had not gone well. The CFO had initially been dismissive of him, making him stand outside his office door while he returned phone calls. Then, when Max had finally been allowed to enter and ask his few questions, the man had again been curt and sarcastic in his replies, turning aside the inquiries, saying, "Why do you need that? Why do you need to 'read' the general ledger anyway? The printed summaries I prepared—and that Nell delivered—should satisfy any auditor's needs for general ledger information. You need to concentrate your efforts on the balance sheet accounts. You don't have much time! Besides," he'd hotly continued, "the information I gave you is what the investment bankers are expecting. They are looking for confirmation of balance sheet amounts, such as receivables, payables, and fixed assets, and are hardly interested in the income statement above the bottom line. Do you understand? My summaries are quite adequate for that conclusion—you need nothing more!" He'd then glowered at the young accountant as if to challenge him to dispute his words. "And you and Minz *will* be out of here within two weeks," he'd vowed, still scowling and tapping the desk with his pencil. "Ten workdays ..."

• • •

"... should satisfy the auditor's information needs." Max had heard the words, and the challenge. And he had surprised himself: he kept his cool. *How 'bout that?* He was glad he'd made the effort. *Motivating.*

He had padded back across the wide lobby, returning to his tiny room and the massive stack of general ledger pages. "So I'll use what I got. Probably be gone come Friday anyway." He'd started with the wide pages where the expense accounts appeared to begin. *Let's see—salaries and wages...*

• • •

Nell couldn't bring Max the invoice copies he'd requested. "Not this afternoon. Too busy now," she explained. "Tomorrow. Friday. Maybe I could get them for you tomorrow," she halfway promised.

"You know, Nell, I could come to your office now and pull my own invoices—if that would help," he offered. *Begged.*

"Um, yeah—no—maybe. But I'll need to get Howard's—Mr. Fleet's—approval first ... and, um, he's, um, left for the day." She sounded stressed.

He was irritated.

"Tell you what, Nell. It's late, and I don't want to leave your stuff in my office overnight anyway. So let's wait till tomorrow, and I'll have Randal Minz do the asking ... instead of either me or you. What say?" He could almost feel her immediate relief radiate through the phone.

"Great!" she brightly agreed. "In fact, if you don't mind, just leave your original requests on the chair outside my door ... when you leave. You're not staying much longer, are you? See, I have an appointment—my hair—and Howard asked me to stay—"

"As long as the auditor is still here," Max said, finishing her sentence. "No, I'm about ready to leave now, too. I'll walk over in a minute and put my list on your chair at your office. OK?"

"Sure, sure," she gushed. She wondered now why Howard had said what he did about this guy. He didn't seem at all like such a bad person—someone to be wary of should he ask for information. Still, she wished her boss was here to guide her. "And to review those damned invoices he's requested," she muttered as she hung up the phone. Lying to the auditor just now about her state of busyness bothered her somewhat, but her boss had definitely made it clear about giving the young man anything prior to his review of the requested items. "But I'm not giving him anything now," she reasoned. "Besides, Howie will really appreciate my hair tonight … for sure." She smiled with certainty.

She and Fleet had begun dating soon after she'd been hired as his assistant, and over subsequent months, they'd become very close. "I just hope he notices my hair before he tries unzipping my dress. And tonight … may be the night," she sang in a whisper to herself. She'd expected Howard to have "popped the question" before now, maybe even months ago, even though he'd often cautioned her that they might have to wait until the company's stock sale was complete—and he was in charge of VisualOptics as the new chief executive officer. He'd said they should keep their relationship secret—especially from Mr. Walton—until the investment bankers had firmed up the final financing arrangements "to avoid certain complications." But he'd not specified anything more about these complications—*because that information is probably over my head anyway*, she reasoned. And, tonight, she was in love, and her man was taking her to a very nice place in Tampa (they were not frequenting the local nightclubs and restaurants either). "But soon, very soon," she sang.

She switched off her calculator and rechecked her desk drawers, making sure they were securely latched and locked. She then stood and made her way around the desk to the bank of file cabinets against the wall, clearing her work files from the tops of the cabinets as she walked.

"So where are you going to put this stuff?" she asked herself. Her arms were full, and she was running late for her appointment. "Here." She dropped the stack of files onto a nearby chair and unlocked the last file cabinet, the one with the empty drawers on the bottom. She'd sort through the mess tomorrow and re-file all the folders in the morning. "Just receipts anyway."

One minute and thirty seconds later, she was striding across the sidewalk toward her car in the reserved parking area. She'd spied no other employees through the tall windows along the front when she'd crossed the lobby and had forgotten her intention to reconfirm the audit guy's departure status.

"Thank heavens—no Mexicans," she breathed. She hated it when the dark men would linger in the lot, gazing after her when she passed. She knew exactly what they were thinking.

Meanwhile, back in the tiny office, the audit guy heard the exit door whoosh shut. He stood and sauntered over to the doorway, checking for any new arrivals and, perhaps, the returning CFO. He had told Nell he would soon be leaving for the day but he'd forgotten this last worksheet, the one adding documentation sources to his sampling of employee expense reports. It was an easy task, and he'd hoped to complete this last workpaper before Randal arrived tomorrow—so his boss could do the final step: obtaining the source documents and other evidential matter for the sampled transactions. The files he'd been given, the ones Fleet had earlier directed to be stacked on his desk, contained none of the source material he needed. "So I'll just let ol' Howard browbeat Randal when he asks for the receipts. Or maybe not." An uneasy feeling then crossed his stomach: the thought that maybe Minz wouldn't support him, maybe saying they really should limit their ticking and tying to just those furnished files. "After all, the fee is a big one," he told himself, "and Randal needs this audit. And maybe he won't approve of my method of statistical sampling anyway ...

because it is kind of new." *Ah well.* "Tomorrow will be my last day anyway."

Through the glass doors, he caught sight of Nell hurrying across the roadway toward her parked car. "Whoa! That girl has a definite way to her walk. Quite a posterior there—like two cats fighting under a blanket." That had been one of his father's favorite sayings and—"Uh-oh!" He immediately grimaced; he was talking aloud to himself, and there could be other employees standing close by. He slowly pivoted in place, surveying the wide lobby and the offices far across the way. "Nope. Dark. You're all by yourself, boy," he affirmed. "Whew!"

Now glancing off in the other direction, toward his right and the steel double doors, he suddenly felt the urge to stroll back to see if any of the other employees were still at work in the warehouse. "I wonder if ..." Maybe he'd search for the manager, to ask him why he'd scarcely made an appearance around him since they'd talked days before? "I know ol' Fleet told those guys to stay away from us—me," he muttered, "but you'd think ol' Rolando'd at least pass by and wave through the door. Maybe just to check on the boys' work on my paint job.

"Or maybe not." Just as quickly, he changed his mind, deciding that such a meeting could wait until tomorrow; he wanted to first finish that workpaper on his desk. "And afterward to drop by our accounting offices." Thinking about the damage to his car had reminded him he'd still not talked with Gordon. "To jack him up, by gosh! Got to be done while I can. Almost forgot ... so much has happened." He shook his head and turned back to his desk and his sampling workpaper.

• • •

Soon, the worksheet was complete, and Max was ready for the next day. "Randal can look over the accounts himself tomorrow to see if I missed any transactions he wants traced. Hah!" He scoffed at the thought: *That isn't going to happen.* "If anything, Randal will strike off about half those entries I selected for tracing and testing. He'd probably been happy with Howard's general ledger summaries. Hah!"

He ran his finger down the column of invoice numbers he wanted to review. *About four hundred, I guess.* He knew the tracing and review phase would take a couple days and that his boss might object to the required effort. And hadn't Fleet reminded him this morning that the entire on-site audit was scheduled for only two weeks? *Very short time for such a big company,* he thought. *Ah well. It's time to go anyway. Put your stuff away.* To his surprise, he found he was actually feeling some reluctance in packing up because he also felt ... *curious.* He couldn't think of a better word. He'd selected transactions from the huge volume, and now he wanted to study how they were grouped and accumulated in the general ledger. He wanted to see the flow of costs and to flesh out the stories behind the need to incur such costs. He'd noted trends and repetitions of sums and vendor names that demanded further study and illumination. *Sleuth?* He wanted to see, to understand, the routine financial guts of the company. *Ah well,* he sighed again. He was alone; Nell had gone for the day; there was no one to retrieve the papers he needed. *As if Howard's gonna give them all to me anyway.* Another sigh. He clicked shut the locks on his case and hefted it. *Heavy.* Even though he'd stowed away whole groups of uncompleted, ring-bound work papers in the spaces beneath the credenza's drawers, there were still many more sheets he hadn't wanted to leave in the office overnight. *Sensitive procedures. Probably just being paranoid!* He snorted at his own joke. While he had not detected any signs of someone having rummaged through his stuff while he was away from the desk, he also hadn't allowed much unattended time to occur: he no longer journeyed to the employee lounge for lunch, and his infrequent bathroom breaks had been brief.

He pulled his office door to, turned the key, and rattled the lock. Then, after stashing his heavy audit bag just inside the glass doors at the front, he crossed the lobby to Nell's office to deliver his information-request pages. Out of habit, he tried her door. *Open?* The doorknob turned easily in his hand. He cautiously tapped the door inward so it didn't bang against the wall and looked about the room. *No one here.* Nell's desk was totally cleared of papers and files. *Not even pictures.* "Looks like a page in a catalog," he observed. "The girl even cleans off the tops of her filing cabinets. Wow! Gotta be for Fleet—his orders."

He leaned farther into the room. Even though the early evening's murky light still filtered through the open doorway from the tall glass windows at the front, he flipped the switch on the wall there beside his hand: the overhead rows of fluorescent lamps instantly flared; he had to momentarily shield his eyes. "Whoa! Bright!" His vision had adjusted to the lobby's light level as he'd walked over. "Just take a minute ... that's better."

He stepped inside. "Now, I wonder if ..." He sauntered over to the closest set of file cabinets and tried the button under the top drawer's handle. "Open. Well, what do you know? Ol' Nell forgot to lock this cabinet as well as her door. What do you know?" He turned, re-surveying the open lobby through the door: He confirmed he was still alone.

He turned back to the file cabinet and eased open the top drawer. "Hmm." He leafed through the tabs on the hanging folders and immediately noticed the codes at the end of the label names: "All like blocks of numbers on the green-screen printouts. Now supposing ..." He wondered if perhaps these files contained the invoices and supporting documents for general ledger accounts. "It'd make sense, wouldn't it?" He closed the top drawer and opened the second. *Same thing.* And then the third. Only the bottom drawer had no files hanging in the racks. "Just some interesting-looking correspondence files," he murmured. These were the files Nell had hastily scooped from atop the cabinets and dumped in the bottom drawer.

"You know, I bet this is part of the stuff I'll be asking for tomorrow. Maybe I should follow up where I can tonight and save myself some time tomorrow?" he rationalized. "No one should mind. And it'll help Nell, too. Save her from picking through the folders looking for dates and such and then making copies and then carrying them to me way over there." He glanced back again, across the wide empty lobby, toward the closed door of his office. "You know, I'll just grab my stuff ... and work right here." *Save time.* The decision made, he retraced his steps across the terrazzo to the entrance door to retrieve his case, his quick steps thumping in the still air. "It's convenient, and she has a calculator, too," he reasoned, nodding to the room. "And I'm not getting in anybody's way either." *Words of defense.* In truth, he suspected the CFO might very well object to his working after hours in the assistant's office—unsupervised and unattended.

Back again in Nell's office, Max pulled the coffee table and then the low cushioned chair around beside the cabinets. *There.* He carried her calculator to the table, and he was ready for work. And the hours flew by.

● ● ●

The outer room now in deep shadow, Max was having trouble reading the small print on the slips of paper he'd spread on the surface of the coffee table. "Should be like the others," he complained. "Smaller type or something. Doesn't foot to the total." He'd begun his review about two hours earlier and had rapidly made his way down his lists, locating and pulling available files from the tall cabinet. As he'd expected, the filing system's numbers mirrored those printed on the green-screen pages; he'd had little trouble locating the sought-after folders. But now he'd reached the employees' expense reports, and he was having some difficulty in reconciling the receipts enclosed in the envelopes, the expense reports, with the numbers on the front. Specifically, he'd selected Nell's expense report for May, and, for some reason, it appeared that she'd been paid an additional four hundred dollars for the month. He'd already retrieved her April expense envelope, and it, too, had been over-reimbursed by exactly four hundred dollars. *This is definitely not good.* His breaths came faster. "There's Fleet's initials at the bottom. He footed it; he approved it."

Max stood and pulled out the top drawer. He flipped through the rack searching for Howard's folder. *Getting dark outside. Gotta hurry.* But he couldn't seem to locate the manila file. *Not here. Not in order.* He sat back down in the low chair. *Maybe here in the bottom.* He'd noticed a pile of unfiled papers in the bottom drawer. Rolling it fully open, he immediately spotted Fleet's thick folder. *On top. Convenient.* Lifting it from the drawer, he flipped it facedown on the table; he'd first look through the contents, oldest to newest, back to front. *New York, New York, Chicago, New York, New Orleans—wonder what that trip was about?* As he sorted through the pile of envelopes, a single sealed package for each of Fleet's business trips with a copy of the reimbursement check neatly stapled to the front, he fingered the contents through the paper. *Just more paper.* He was impressed with the CFO's method of keeping track of his expenses. *Very neat. Too neat?*

He retrieved Nell's folder from his pile and noted that she'd not completed such an envelope during the entire year. *Must be that she doesn't travel.* Her file contained receipts for office supplies, receipts from local restaurant—the stuff he'd expect in any secretary's expense folder—all bound together and crowned with an adding-machine tape that tied to the reimbursement amount (except for the additional four hundred dollars). *Let Randal ask about that sum in the morning.*

Returning to Fleet's pile of receipts, Max selected another package with a reference number that tied to his test-sample listing. Because the CFO's apparent travel was so extensive—and expensive—several of his envelopes had been selected via the audit-sampling procedure. *I betcha ol' Howard's gonna be quite upset with me ... but what difference will that make?* He scarcely hesitated before running his thumb along the glued flap.

"OK, sports fans. What do we have here? Airfares, gas receipts, hotel receipts, meal receipts—all documented with names and dates and purposes." The documentation looked very good—*supportive*. Max compared the receipts with the front page. *Easy to read, too. Even has the same ink throughout.* "Ol' Howard must favor a certain pen for filling out his expense reports. Wonder why he doesn't have a company credit card?"

Max thumbed open the second selected envelope. *Airfares, gas receipts, hotel receipts, meal receipts—all the same thing.* He flipped over the envelope and compared the line entries. *All OK.* The auditor was very impressed. *Better than textbook illustrations.* Then he saw it: the numbers on the gas receipts. "Consecutive!" Howard's gas receipts were consecutively numbered! *Now how often does that happen?*

"All the time if you have your own pad of receipts," he answered himself.

He reopened the first envelope; the gas receipts there were also consecutively numbered. "Interesting." It was going to be a long night. He called Randal's house.

• • •

Friday morning, Max parked his car close to the fence—about the same place where he'd parked the previous morning. He'd selected the spot not so much because he was a creature of habit—because he was—but because he could see the entire parking lot from there and could remain somewhat inconspicuous on the open range of the vast parking area. At the moment, however, his car was the only car in the lot, and the chain-link fence cast little of the covering shadow he'd anticipated.

"Shouldn't matter anyway," he told himself. As the sun now lightened the eastern skies, his boss arrived. "And Randal's on time for once. How 'bout that?" He watched the Jag's high beams slowly sweep across the parking lot, revealing his vehicle on the first pass.

Randal accelerated, circling wide to line up his car a safe distance from the aging Chevy. He braked to a smooth stop, killed his lights, and dismounted; Max met him at the rear.

"Morning, boss."

"Morning, kiddo. You know, you didn't have to park way out here on the North Forty. These damned pebbles probably chipped the hell outta my paint."

Max snorted his reply: "Typical. Here we've got crime and conspiracy in our midst, and you're worried about a little dust getting on your car. Hah!"

"Well … " Randal let the comment pass unchallenged; he could barely see Max's face in the faint illumination from the distant streetlights spaced along US 19; his steely-eyed glare would be wasted on the boy.

"So then, you think you've caught Howard and his girlfriend stealing from the company, huh?" he growled instead. "Maybe we should see what you've got, kiddo, before we start making accusations? OK?" Without waiting for an answer, Randal wheeled toward the sprawling grayness that was the VisualOptics building and crunched off across the parking lot at a brisk pace. "Come on," he called back over his shoulder. "Keep up. We'll wait at the door. You can tell me more about what you think you've uncovered while we walk. John Walton's going to be here soon. We're going to discuss this with him before Howard arrives."

Max squinted his displeasure; he was confused. *Randal sounded so friggin' different on the phone last night. Alarmed. Interested. Encouraging.* He hurried to catch up with the man. *Dang Randal! He's not carrying a friggin' thing, and I'm lugging this forty-pound audit bag. And the guy's irritated with me now?* "Hey, wait up," he puffed. "I can't talk and run at the same time."

His boss slowed until he caught up. He began again; between deep, measured breaths, he recounted yesterday's findings as they trudged forward: the receipts—the consecutive ones for gas and the suspicious-looking ones he'd noticed later in the evening, after he'd talked with Randal (mostly hotels and restaurants)—and the regular payments to Nell (unsubstantiated). He finished about the same time they reached the sidewalk at the building's entrance. "Any questions?"

"Nope," Randal simply replied. He walked on and leaned against the door, pressing his face to the thick glass and cupping his eyes with his hands as he searched the lobby. "Say, did you see anybody arrive ahead of you? I think there's somebody moving around inside."

Max gasped. *Fleet!* His first thought was that the man had arrived sometime during the night, noticed the open cabinets and misplaced folders, and decided to do a bit of evidence destruction. *Dang!* He wished now he'd spent the night in the parking lot as he'd suggested to Randal on the phone—but his boss had vetoed the idea. "You're not double oh seven," he'd said. "I'd probably be bailing you out of jail in the middle of the night if the cops were to happen by."

"Oh crap! What if Fleet came back and—"

Then, suddenly, new lights passed over them as another vehicle turned in from the road, following the asphalt roadway around to the front of the building. It pulled into the first reserved parking space and stopped. Quiet returned.

"Well, it looks like Mr. Fleet *is* here with us," Randal wryly observed. "That's his car. Now this could be awkward."

Click! The glass door unlocked behind them, and John Walton pushed open the door. "Coffee's on," he announced. "You boys want a cup?"

"Oh damn!" Max muttered. This was all happening too fast.

Randal chuckled. "Nothing ever goes completely according to plan, boy, especially when you're auditing. And if you don't have your ducks lined up right, you sometimes get hard lessons." He patted Max's shoulder. "But I'm betting you've got your ducks lined up perfectly." He raised his chin to the shadowy figure approaching from the parked car. "Good morning to you, Howard," he loudly greeted. "You certainly keep early morning hours."

"Got a lot to do," he snarled. "And you guys have a lot of work to do—and a week to do it in." If the CFO had been alarmed by this early-morning visitation, he hid it well. He brushed by and nodded to Walton at the door. "And I thought you were supposed to be in Atlanta today?"

"Got a lot of work to do," John evenly replied, "maybe like you."

Fleet halted in the open doorway, turning slightly to study his chief executive officer's face in the faint light. Besides happening on an unannounced committee convening at dawn, he seemed to have caught something different in the CEO's voice. He heard something unfinished, as if Walton had more to say.

"So what the hell's going on?" he demanded.

"Well, let's find out together," John amiably replied. "In my office with these gents."

"OK." Fleet nodded. "OK then," he said and stalked on, through the darkened lobby toward the executive offices.

"And what the hell is this!" The tall man had apparently just noticed the fluorescent light spilling through Nell's open office door along with her mostly open file cabinets. He slowed and veered off in that direction for a closer inspection.

John turned back to the auditors. "You boys might have to wait for that coffee," he opined, pushing wide the door for them to follow.

Moments later, Howard strode into the CEO's office, his hands balled in fists, his mouth set in a firm line. "What the hell is this?" he demanded again. The chief financial officer appeared ready to do battle.

Max stood waiting, his mouth as dry as cotton. He'd expected a private morning: a presentation of his workpapers to Randal, who, in turn, would quietly examine them together with the source documentation and offer suggestions to his reasoning or perhaps point out shortcomings in his analysis—a nice, civil little critique like back in Gene McVeigh's class on auditing techniques and principles. But his boss had plopped himself down on a soft chair after first aligning it alongside John's desk. In turn, the CEO had passed behind, patting Randal's shoulder in passing, and eased himself into the huge leather chair behind the desk. They both now rolled back in their chairs, their tucked chins hidden behind steepled fingers, their noncommittal eyes gazing up at him.

Noting the direction of their attentions, Howard likewise turned, swiveling heel and toe, to face the gulping accountant. "So what the hell is this about?" he again asked/demanded.

Max took a deep breath and puffed his cheeks, exhaling. He dropped his eyes from Fleet's hot gaze, searching for a place to seat himself. *Couch or chair? Chair—it's higher.* If he was about to be fired, he didn't want to have to struggle to extricate himself from some cushy piece of furniture. He had his pride.

Lowering his audit case to the carpet and himself to the chair, he popped apart the bag's double locks and flipped open its panels. Reaching inside, he lifted a single manila folder. He again rose to his feet and, stepping around Fleet, handed the file directly to Mr. Walton.

Randal looked on, shifting in his seat and raising himself slightly, trying to study the papers from the side.

"It's a listing of questionable source documents ... that we must discuss," Max smoothly stated, returning to his chair as the papers were spread across the desktop. "As an auditor, I'm here looking for resolution. Explanation." He didn't say "conclusion" at this time; he would not destroy his avenues of retreat. "Gentlemen, I would—"

He stopped midsentence and looked up to the red-faced Fleet. "Howard, would you like to take a seat, too?"

The CFO's nostrils flared with a sharp, angry inhalation. "What?"

"A chair ... there. Or the couch. I can't think while you stand over me. Please."

Deciding he maybe *did* look overly defensive—when he had yet to be accused of anything—and, perhaps, stupid, standing there in the middle of the room, clenching and unclenching his fists, Fleet chose one of the remaining chairs, pushing it around to the far side of Walton's desk, aligning himself with the others.

With their sitting and staring forward, the trio appeared much like a jury—a united band of listeners—as they waited for the accountant. And Max noticed. Swallowing with some effort, he began again, "During the course of my audit—"

"Where did you get those numbers?" Fleet interrupted; he was studying the paper in John's hand. "And invoices, if that's what they are." He was an intelligent man, an accomplished accountant also gifted with excellent eyesight; he could easily read and interpret the workpapers. He was also, in that instant, a very pale man—before he once again became a red and raging one. "That shit wasn't on those schedules I gave you! Where'd you get that detail? Those invoice numbers? Did Nell—did you get anything from our files that you were not specifically given by Nell?" His tone became an accusation.

But Max had noticed the moment of pallor and was encouraged. *Touched a nerve, did I? Now to keep the heat on.* He didn't want Fleet to twist the discourse around to where he had to defend himself—about his rights of access and such. *This isn't a legal proceeding ... yet.* "Howard," he quietly replied, "you gave me those financial records. Your secretary, Nell, gave me directly only what you gave her. Those numbers are your numbers."

"Oh? That's not true! I gave you account summaries and internal analyses?" He didn't challenge the identification of Nell's position as his secretary. "I did not give you anything like that! You did not have that level of detail unless ..." He remembered the huge printout he'd directed Information Services to dump at the office door while the accountant was away for lunch. And it *was* a dump—a complete data dump. "But—but there was no formatting in that report," he protested. "It was just lines and lines of numbers!" He knew that detail for a fact because he'd quickly examined the tall stack of green screen paper before he'd shipped it over. There was no way in the world, he had assured himself, that this fresh-faced neophyte could scrap meaning from these pages.

"And even if you had transaction details," he continued, "that's just numbers. You'd still have to do your ticking and tying. So what's that 'gas receipts' note right there?" Fleet had risen to his feet and hovered over Walton's shoulder, pointing as he studied the sheets in the folder. "How many pages do you have here?" He attempted to pull the papers from beneath John's hand, but stubby fingers pinned them tight. "Um ... and those notes there about hotel locations and dates of stay—my dates of stay. Unless you'd gotten the receipts ..."

Howard's voice faded. He suddenly connected the meaning of Nell's open office door and the extended file-cabinet drawers. *This asshole's been through my files!* "This asshole's been through my files!" he blurted. "That's—that's trespassing! John, I'm going to call the police!"

"Fleet, sit down!" Walton ordered, his shouted command ringing in the room. "Max has hardly said a word, and you're ready to call the police? Not hardly. Now sit down and shut up!"

Howard sat, his eyes darting to and fro across the floor; he sulked. John Walton had never dared to talk like that to him before. He was too valuable! He was needed!

"OK," Max started again. "See, those gas receipts supporting Mr. Fleet's business auto usage are all consecutively numbered—which is not likely from my experience." (His experience was limited to those few trips when Randal had given him cash for the gas to run errands for the office.) "Someone must have a pad of those things. And those hotel receipts? Fake. I pulled a salesman's receipts that I'd selected in another sample—same hotel chain—and they don't use those receipt forms anymore. So I called the hotel's head office last night. They said someone was using forms that had been discontinued years ago." He was being careful to say "someone" and not Fleet. "And, um, I noticed additional sums, approved by Mr. Fleet, being regularly paid to Nell and ... that were not documented." *I'd better be real careful now.* "And I noticed, in the file cabinet, certain letters to her from—"

"I'm calling the police right now!" Howard shouted, lunging to his feet and racing out the door. He turned to his left, heading back to Nell's office where he suspected she'd squirreled away more of his little notes and invites. *If I told her once, I told her a million times! Don't keep paper!* He skidded to a stop before the long row of file cabinets. Kneeling as he slammed shut the empty bottom drawer in the first cabinet, he wrenched open the second drawer where he knew his expense-report folders were stored. *Gone.* Someone had taken his files! "Maybe Nell moved them," he whispered.

"Howard," John softly called from the open doorway. "I've got your expense folders in my office. And I've got the correspondence files from Nell's desk. I know what you've been telling those bankers, and I know what you and Nell got going on. Gosh, boy, I think you got more of my letters in your files than I got in mine. And that little ol' gal's been serving you fine for quite a while now—and I mean servicing, too." The old man was shaking his head; his face was grim. There was no humor intended.

"John, you don't understand!" Fleet struggled to his feet. "I can explain everything. Don't believe what you're hearing from that sniveling auditor. I can explain everything!"

"Great," John simply replied. "If you need it, take the rest of the day and figure out just what you *can* explain. And then, Monday, I'll arrange for the board to meet. You can do a little 'splainin'—as Ricky says to Lucy—to them, too. Meantime, these boys here will continue with their auditing and will get their reports direct from IS. And I'll see if I can get Nell some help in retrieving files, and, eh, she should work through me today. Only me. OK? And then we'll decide what else we need to do on Monday."

Walton turned to leave and then turned back. He motioned to his side, and another man stepped into view in the doorway; it was Rolando. "Howard, one other thing: I know you fired this fellow from his warehouse job ... but I've hired him back. He mentioned he has some military security work in his background, so he'll be transitioning over to heading up our security folks—seeing as how I don't know the extent of the present guy's relationship with you. And ol' Rolando here will be staying with you today, shadowing you and making sure you don't destroy any files or such and that you hand over your keys to him before you go home tonight. Understand?"

Fleet nodded weakly.

An hour later, Rolando watched him leave the building; he didn't return.

• • •

"Can you boys use a fresh cup?" John was standing at the door of the tiny office holding a steaming pot of coffee. "I made another batch. I think I'll be here awhile more."

Randal looked up from behind the desk. (After lunch, he'd commandeered Max's cushy office chair, complaining that his working at the folding table in a straight-backed chair was killing his spine.) "Coffee? Umm, no, no, better not," he decided. "If I drink any more tonight, I won't be able to sleep."

At the table, Max held out his cup. "Thanks, I'd appreciate some. Say, you going to be here awhile?"

"Yeah," John said, his voice tired, resigned. "When you find a man being dishonest with the small stuff, you'll usually find he's been dishonest with the big stuff, too."

"That what you're finding?" Randal asked, rolling back from the desk. "Did you go through his drawers and file cabinets already?" That was what he'd suggested Walton do at the first opportunity.

"Yeah—me and ol' Rolando. We went through every drawer in Howard's office. Surprisingly, he's kept few written documents in his files."

"You know you have other help, too: the chief accountant ... and Nell?"

"Nell didn't show up today, Randal. I didn't think she would. I bet that's why Howard left so quickly this morning: he wanted to call her. And, yeah, I've got other accounting help. The chief accountant, Harold—you've met him, Max—and the other guys said they can handle things." John looked about for a place to deposit the coffeepot, setting it on the table after he'd cleared a spot. "Yeah," he continued, "the accounting folks actually seem, well, *happy* that Fleet's left and hasn't come back. They said they could handle things fine." He fell silent for the moment, arranging his thoughts as he stared at the floor. "And I think we should push back our financing plans." He looked up again, his eyes newly bright, intense. "You know, Randal, I talked to the investment bankers, and they were under the impression that this 'going public' deal would leave Fleet owning a sizable portion of the company's stock. They said they were told that *he'd* be the CEO and that I'd be retiring." Walton's eyes blazed. "And, you know, when I talked with a few of the older board members, they let me know they'd had some concerns about Fleet and several of the newer board members—those folks the investment bankers *demanded* we add—per Howard." He sighed heavily and returned to staring at the floor and shaking his head.

"I've been a total fool," he said, his voice low. "A total fool."

Silence. Randal cleared his throat. "You're an honest man, John," he said. "A trustworthy man, and you assume others are like you—until you know different. And Howard is a very intelligent man who trusts no one. He's a bully, and I expect we'll find a lot of employees here who are—were—terrified of him."

"He's probably a bit of a psychopath, too," Max added. Both men turned their faces to him, as if questioning his term. "See," he explained, "Howard's probably devoid of guiding moral standards and principles—honesty, truthfulness, compassion, the stuff we normally expect to find in others—so he's probably not conflicted about hiding guilt and such. He could concentrate his efforts; he's not distracted like we'd be. So, in a way, he's freer to do what we couldn't imagine." He glanced at Randal. "Or, at least, what I couldn't imagine," he corrected himself.

Randal snorted. "Had me fooled, too, kiddo," he laughed.

John laughed, too. "If I understood correctly, I think you got a point there, boy," he said, retrieving his coffeepot from the table. "If you don't believe you're doing anything different—or wrong— then there ain't any 'tells,' as they say in gambling circles. You've had a psychology class or two in college, son?"

"Abnormal," Max confirmed, smiling. "Speaking of which," he said, turning back to Randal, "I really should be going. I wanted to stop by the office tonight. I need to speak with Gordon about—"

"Gone."

"What?"

"Gone," Randal repeated. "I fired him earlier this week. I heard about what he did to your car—Lou told me. That was a really cowardly thing to do, you know."

Max puffed his cheeks, clearly surprised by the news.

Another silent second passed. John shuffled his feet, standing there in the doorway. "Well," he announced, "I guess I've had enough excitement for the day. And it's clear you boys got lots more to do, so ... adios." He waved over his shoulder as he turned from the room, returning to his own office across the way.

They watched after him.

"Randal," Max said, his voice soft, reflective, "about Gordon. I'd hate to think I was the cause of another man losing his job. I mean, I appreciate your concern for me and all, and, you know, I hate to think I could be causing more work and difficulty for you, but ..." He glanced back to the desk: Randal was focused on his examination of the tip of his little finger, searching for evidence of earwax deposits. "Randal?" He then realized his boss had actually been looking for a way to ease the fat man out of the firm. "You were going to fire him anyway, weren't you? Weren't you?"

"Yeah," he simply agreed. "End of tax season and all. Say, think you can work this weekend?"

• • •

The next week, Max would receive two letters.

He'd find the first one on his car's dashboard, surrounded by glass from the smashed windshield. The second would arrive in his mailbox. Both would convey similar messages: "You've destroyed my life, and I'll get even somehow. I want to kill you," and "You're dead, asshole." Max would guess the first letter to be from Howard.

CHAPTER 3

ALMOST NOON

"**S**o what do you think, Detective Bryce?" I ask. She's finished the top packet and is reexamining the threat letters stapled to it, stroking her chin as she mulls over the chapter. I notice she's also gotten a good tan from her vacation time. It suits her.

"Well, I'm not so sure that accountants should be allowed to write books," she says. "At least I hope mine never does."

"Yeah, but other than that, do you think there's relationship potential with our case? Serious potential?"

"'You've destroyed my life,'" Allison reads aloud, "'and I'll get even somehow. I want to kill you,' and 'You're dead, asshole.'" She thumbs her glasses to the bridge of her nose and leans back in her squeaky chair. "Yes, Detective Eltie, I'd say serious potential does exist and that we should look up the offended ones. They could still feel aggrieved and could possibly wish a measure of harm to befall Mr. Anderson." She frowns and shakes her head. "Damn! I'm beginning to sound like you!"

I laugh. "So maybe we check on 'em—see what they've been up to?" She nods her agreement, peering over the tops of her glasses.

"What about Airman Thacker?" I ask, only half teasing. "Him, too?"

Allison exhales loudly, her eyelids lower in thought. "Well, let's see ..." She leans forward again and begins riffling through the pages. "June 1975 ... Vietnam would've been winding down in '73

… unlikely Mr. Thacker would have remembered Mr. Anderson from boot camp days and even less likely he'd …" Her voice trails off as she locates and smooths the *Times* clipping on the desk in front of her. "There." She scans down the page. "As I was saying, unlike certain persons in the VisualOptics chapter, I hadn't remembered reading about him in the newspaper article as a character who could be considered poked, as you'd say, or provoked, as I would say. In fact, he's barely mentioned in the decedent's writing. So he probably wouldn't have felt threatened by anything in the article—even if Anwain Thacker was his real name." She holds up the full-page newsprint. "Besides, he'd be a bit long in the tooth now—as you'd also say—along with Nell, Howard, *and* Gordon."

"I agree—as *you'd* say. So, um, read another one, another chapter in his book. I got lots of stuff I should do right now before …" It's almost lunchtime already. "Maybe we could go get a bite to eat in a little while?"

Allison pauses before answering, consulting her mental to-do list again. "OK … sure." She nods. "So then, do you have any suggestions?"

I brighten.

"Reading suggestions," she hurriedly adds, turning the *Times* article toward me and tapping the paper with the pen she takes from the cup on my desk. "I mean reading suggestions. Maybe this one about the chicken processor and the freezers packed with—what's that say?—dog carcasses?"

"No, no." I roll my chair back and cross my arms. "Well, yes, it does say dog carcasses, but there's a better one there you should read first—at least before lunch. Ironically,"—I appreciate irony, even when I have to point it out—"I remember something about that story, or an occurrence remarkably similar to it—since we're dealing with professed fictional accounts." I smile with the thought. *More irony?* "In that particular chapter, it seems ol' auditor Max happened on a cache of canine dressed for the market while he was counting inventory in the freezers of a huge chicken processor ... headquartered in Lakeland, I believe." The newspaper hadn't actually revealed a location in the article; that's just my remembrance. "Anyway, the company I remember was sold in the eighties to an Arkansas conglomerate, and the owner—if that's who Max fashions as the primary character in the story—ended up in poverty ... and deceased. I checked; he'd passed away some twenty years ago. Now, as to whether or not Max played a role in causing that distress sale, I'd have to—"

"Did he also leave a threat note?" Allison asks. She's flipping through the stapled packets again.

"Yeah. It's the one written in Chinese—or Korean maybe. But I didn't bother with a translation of it since the company's owner has long since expired and couldn't have been involved in Anderson's murder. Besides, he'd apparently chased ol' Max around the freezer with just a large sword—not a shotgun—after he'd asked about the absence of valuable dog steaks in the inventory count sheets. The old fellow had, for some reason, thought the auditor was ready to disclose his hobby activities together with the company's financials; he didn't know he was kidding. Then the health department decided to visit that same day. Hah! All purely coincidental ... according to the story."

"Funny." She chuckles.

"Yeah, it was ... unless you were selling meat to restaurants back then."

She laughs again. "Oh, I don't know. It could have been a draw—meaning more business. Fricassee au Fido? Or Roasted Rover maybe?"

"Allison—"

"Remember that time you ate alligator tail in front of me? Couldn't have been any worse."

"Allison—"

"OK, sir. Which story *do* you suggest I read next then? The corrupt political party chairwoman? The pot-smuggling boatbuilder?

Maybe the Louisiana alligator salesmen? The—what's that?—olive-oil mafia?"

"Eh, yeah, yeah, read that one." My rumbling stomach agrees. "There's more to that story than ol' Max even knew about." I vaguely gesture toward the photo of the pistol. "It's a short chapter, too."

CHAPTER 4
AUGUST 1978

Knock, knock, knock!

KMax jumped in his seat; the sudden sound startled him. He fumbled with his eyeglasses, straightening them while focusing in on the source of the disturbance: a guy pounding on his door—one of the junior accountants. "Gosh, Warren! You scared the crap outta me! Whew! 'Bout gave me a heart attack."

Standing in the doorway, Warren Schmotz smiled broadly, bobbing as he inwardly laughed—his trademark silent chuckle, as they called it in the office. "Got a minute?" he asked.

Max waved in the man, saying, "Come in, come in. Take a seat. You about ready to go home? Or did you just stop by to help me soil my skivvies?"

"Hah!" Warren snorted aloud this time. "Thanks. I needed that. But ..." His face then turned serious. "No, I've—I wanted to tell you I've handed in my resignation to Randal. I've just come from his office."

"Whoa!" Max huffed with surprise; he hadn't seen this coming. He pushed back in his chair, giving his visitor an openmouthed, astonished expression that changed rapidly to an incredulous one. "You're kidding me, aren't you?" When he'd hired the young accountant, he had expected him to settle into the firm like a glove, to start with the income-tax work and eventually take over some of the auditing tasks. He'd invested much time in training this guy, even taking him along on trips to visit clients, introducing him as his associate as they laid out the various jobs' demands. *Maybe that was it?*

"Eh, you weren't … eh, you aren't frightened by the way Sal and Alex acted this morning, are you?" He had invited Warren to attend a meeting with him in Tarpon Springs to help gather business files from the offices of Christianopolis & Sons, Painting Contractors. The patriarch of the company had recently died, and now the two sons were scuffling over the estate, suing and countersuing each other, both claiming majority control of their enterprise. Minz & Associates, CPAs, PA, had been engaged by Alex Christianopolis's attorney to reconstruct certain accounting records, and Max had asked Warren to accompany him to speed the task—or perhaps, as he'd joked, to provide security should the elder brother, Sal, prove unwilling to keep his telephoned promise of access—and safety. "I mean, those—those Greeks didn't even once whip out knives or anything … not even one time today!" he noted, finishing in a rush. It had been an altogether calm, uneventful, and uncharacteristic meeting. Not like some others he'd attended.

Warren again shook with his silent chuckle, his already-dark complexion deepening a shade. "No, no, it's nothing like that," he said. "See, I've really liked working for you—"

"With," Max interrupted. "With me." He had to lean far back in his chair to look up; Warren was a pretty tall kid—about six two if he had to guess—and built like an athlete. *Maybe that invitation to Tarpon Springs really was for more than just training purposes.*

Warren moved closer, his eyes dropped, his fingertips idly brushing the desk's surface; this conversation was obviously tougher than he'd expected. "OK," he agreed. "'With you.' See, I've really liked working with you for the past year … but, see, I have no long-term prospects with Randal and this firm. This place couldn't be my life's career. Understand?" He shrugged his shoulders and slightly cocked his head to one side, holding forward his open hands as in supplication—another trademark expression. Actually this was a gesture Warren and Randal shared. "Understand?" he asked again.

Max stared hard into the young man's eyes, trying to understand. He shook his head. "No, no, I don't—why not? You're a good accountant. You're progressing in this job—doing better all the time. And you and Randal get along OK. You're both Jewish and ... what?"

Warren was sadly shaking his lowered head. "See, that's it. You don't get it; you don't understand. See, Jews ... Jews often don't work so well for other Jews—or, at least, not for long."

"What?" Max was back to his incredulous stare. "I've never heard that before. Gosh. I'd say it must be confusing in Israel then. Or New York!"

Warren took another deep breath. "Just the same, I need to look further, to try out more things before I settle down, to look around while I still can. And, see, my father has purchased a business for me to run—"

"Ohhh." Suddenly the situation cleared for Max. "Your father—and Randal—and the synagogue ... you're all members of Congregation Beth, aren't you?" He remembered Warren's dad from the last board meeting: the elder Schmotz and Randal Minz had gotten into a rather heated discussion about the use of proceeds from the synagogue's cemetery business and the range of fee assessments for High Holy Days and just about every other aspect of the organization's financial life.

Warren nodded, his lips tight.

"Ah well, I can understand better, I guess," Max concluded. "Tsk-tsk—luckily us Baptists don't usually have enough stuff to argue over. And there's not an attorney among us on the stewardship committee. I even do the pastor's tax return for free." He slouched lower in his chair, now studying his Pentel pencil, rolling it back and forth between his fingers and thumbs. "So what's your ol' man got waiting for you, Warren?"

"Um, olive-oil distribution," he dully replied, as if that were the most normal of occupational endeavors for budding accountants. He was staring at the Pentel, too.

Max glanced up. "Accounting or management?" he asked. "Or maybe the operations—the labor stuff?" He'd bagged lots of groceries himself, back in the day when he'd worked his way through school.

"All—everything. I'll be doing everything."

"So how many employees total?" Max wasn't quite sure he'd heard right.

"Just me. See, the whole operation is really rather simple. We—I have a warehouse over off Ninth Street South, and I convert a large quantity of olive oil into small containers of olive oil." He paused. "It's, um … you know, you'll have to drop by the place, and maybe we can talk some more." He glanced backward, toward the open door, now seemingly concerned he was being overheard—or telling too much. "Here." He slid a business card across the desk.

"Whoa! Nothing slow about you." Max held the card aloft, reading its raised script.

"My father—he had them printed up. That's for the address. For you."

"Oh? OK. So, eh, will you be in for the rest of the week? Working out your notice?"

"Well, I offered, but Randal said my timing was good; I could leave this evening. See, I've already cleaned out my desk … and put my things in my car. He said it'd be OK with you, too."

Max grimaced. *It'd sure as hell be nice if Minz had bothered to walk over to ask for that opinion.* He'd hoped for some staff assistance with the Freeman's Chemicals audit, to perhaps shorten the period of abuse to a manageable one-week stay instead of the usual two. But now that was obviously not to be. He'd have to endure the company's ancient CEO's constant attention—and criticism—one more time. *Maybe I can visit Warren's business tomorrow and put off Freeman for a day?* Last year, the irascible executive had pulled a chair into the controller's tiny office and sat opposite Max at the table, watching him while he worked and reading every upside-down mark, calculation, and comment added to the audit workpapers. *Maybe Warren's hiring?*

"Ah well," he sighed aloud. "Like I said, you're a good numbers guy, and I hate to see you go. But we'll keep in touch. OK? And I'll be sure to drop by your place to see how you're doing—to see what you're doing."

They shook hands, and the young accountant departed, closing the door behind.

Ah shit! Max spied his Pink Pearl eraser and sent it bouncing off the far wall.

• • •

A couple months passed before he found his way down to Warren's new workplace alongside the train tracks.

Max stood outside the huge double doors of the massive windowless cinder-block structure and beat on the hard metal surfaces with the bottoms of his fists. *Wham! Wham! Wham!* He'd seen Warren's late-model Mustang parked there, in front of the loading dock, when he'd pulled in, so he was reasonably certain the man was somewhere inside the building. *Wham! Wham! Wham!* He looked around; the Mustang and his old Biscayne were the only cars in the entire graveled lot. *Wham! Wham! Wham! … Wham!*

"Ah well," he gasped, breathing heavily. "I guess I should have called first." Then suddenly, the dead bolt on the opposite side of the door clanged, and the steel panels screeched apart.

"What say, old man?" Warren greeted through the dark opening. "Can you, um, get through this space?" He gave the steel door another push; his ex-boss appeared to have not lost any weight since he'd last seen him. "See, I don't use this entrance much, and it's kind of heavy."

"Yeah," Max grunted, now assisting with the door sliding, "and I should be taller, too. So tell me, how do you get stuff inside here? Through those doors along the railroad siding?" He'd seen a lone tanker car parked there when he'd turned in from the street.

"Yeah. That's where my olive oil's delivered."

Max squeezed through the opening and helped to reclose the gap. He whistled as he pushed. "Well, now I'm impressed, Warren. You get olive oil delivered by the railroad carload?"

"Yeah. By the carload," he affirmed. "Whew!"

Max straightened, waiting for more explanation—but none seemed to be forthcoming.

"So let me show you the rest of the place," Warren volunteered, taking his visitor by the elbow. "My equipment is back there, toward the rear of the building."

As they walked, he pointed out the stacks of boxes in the center of the warehouse. "See, those are empty cans there—all one-gallon cans—steel cans. And those are boxes of lids. See?" They reached another set of heavy steel doors; these obviously fronted the tracks running alongside the building. "And those are filled containers there in those cardboard boxes along the wall. Awaiting pickup and delivery."

"In freight cars, too?" Max was prepared to be really impressed.

"No, no." Warren chuckled his silent chuckle. "That wouldn't work. We only cover the Tampa Bay region. No, we—I arrange for delivery via truck; the outside loading dock accommodates both rail-car and truck." He turned and pointed to a mix of machinery, PVC pipes, valves, and conveyor belts positioned against the back wall. "See? That's my filling unit. That's where I do my thing." He flipped a switch and turned on the fluorescents suspended over the area. The stainless-steel machinery gleamed back, reflecting the new light.

"Wow! Nice. Your stuff sure looks nice," Max brightly observed. But it really didn't look that nice. While the funnel-shaped equipment appeared freshly washed and sparkling, the concrete floor shined with the sheen of spilled oil, and the conveyer belt was worn and stained. *Bet that floor is slick as owl poop.*

"Gee, thanks," Warren grinned. "Got to be ready for the health department's visit, you know. Now step over here—watch your footing—and I'll show you how it all works." He grasped the CPA's upper arm, guiding him along as he held tight to the conveyer belt with his other hand. "I busted my butt more than a few times when I first started this business."

"I'd imagine," Max said, sliding to a position at the front of the machine, at its control panel and its assorted gauges and dials. "Those rubber boots are probably the appropriate thing to wear, I guess." He'd noticed the younger man's tall fishing waders as he was being pulled along.

"Yeah, well, sometimes oil spills—here, let me show you how this works." Warren waved upward, toward the looming steel funnel. "See, the olive oil is first pumped from the tanker to that holding tank in batches. See there? Then I position the gallon cans on this conveyer belt and take this hose here, and as the cans pass, I fill them with oil. Cap 'em, box 'em, and they're ready for the truck." He clapped invisible dust from his hands.

"Eh, Warren, that's it? You produce only gallon-size cans of olive oil? Whom do you sell them to?" Max remembered his mother usually had olive oil on hand, in the cupboard. But her oil had come in a three-ounce-or-so bottle and was principally used to alleviate earaches in kids. A gallon can would've lasted them years—*decades*.

"Restaurants. We—I sell cases and cases to restaurants. See, they cook with olive oil—in Greek and Italian restaurants. It's good for you," he asserted. "Good for you."

"Uh, yeah!" Max nodded. He was definitely showing his lack of culinary experience and cultural exposure. "Yeah," he agreed again, facing back toward the machine. "I knew that." A minute of silence passed. "So, what's to keep—"

"Customers coming?" Warren anticipated the question. "I have long-term contracts with restaurants all over the area—Pinellas County, Hillsborough County, and Pasco County."

"I was actually going to ask about competition in the olive-oil trade—about how you got those contracts. I don't know that *I* could go out and market and negotiate those things—oh, wait. You said your father bought the business for you guys. Did it come with the contracts?"

Warren sheepishly grinned. "Yeah," he admitted. "That and the equipment and the building lease—it was an in-place deal. It really wasn't that expensive either. And I'm doing very well," he added, his smile now tending toward smugness. "Very well. You see my car outside?"

"Yeah. So what's to keep out competition?" Max wondered, thinking that if the business was so cheap and so profitable, what was to keep other companies—bigger companies with automatic machines and minimum-wage labor—from underbidding the young entrepreneur in the marketplace? He'd certainly seen enough of that with his other clients and the capitalist economy. *I mean, in a flash.*

A long pause followed; he turned to face the young man. "Warren?"

"Well, not everyone is able to purchase olive oil in the open market," he quietly answered, glancing about, again appearing to fear being overheard. "See? It's like this: my father has had this connection in mind for years. When an opening finally appeared, he went to Tampa and met with Mr. Turfcattie or Tortellini or—"

"Trafficanti?" Max interrupted. "Santo Trafficanti?" About two years back, one of their tax clients had borrowed money from the Tampa crime family—and the loan's conditions had turned out to be exceptionally harsh, resulting in an eventual business failure and the client's flight from the state. Randal had talked with Max afterward, telling him of his past encounters with Trafficanti and his limited knowledge of the mobster's tangled affairs. And back then, the stories had felt to him like a gathering of fictions or, at least, the trailer to a good movie—that had been his impression. Now, with the mention of the name, he'd remembered Randal's words. *Not a fiction.* Max felt a chill for his friend. *Maybe the market isn't so open?*

But Warren seemed pleasantly surprised. After all, his ex-boss had appeared to possess scant knowledge of international trade items, cultural foodstuffs, and such. "Yeah!" he exclaimed. "Do you know him? Apparently he and my father know each other from the old country—or maybe it was New York. When my father heard about this opening, this place, he went to see him—Trafficanti. Apparently the guy has cornered the olive-oil trade from Italy, and you've got to get his permission to even order the stuff from there. But you've got to order in such a volume—but it's not hard." He was reconnoitering the place again, his eyes searching in the dark corners.

"Expecting somebody?" Max asked—both a question and an observation. "Maybe I shouldn't be here?"

"No, no. See, my father is dropping by sometime today to pick up the figures … and he—he doesn't like me talking about business with anyone else. You understand how old immigrant people are, don't you?"

"Yeah, my dad wasn't an immigrant, but he was like that: 'Don't tell the other man your business, or he'll know everything you do!' Sound familiar?"

"Yeah." Warren was shaking with a silent chuckle. His smiling teeth were as white as ever.

Max patted him on the shoulder. "Well, you don't have to worry about me telling anyone else about your business," he assured him. "I'm discreet. It goes with the profession, doesn't it? Accounting clients will talk about their sex lives before they'll share financial information, won't they? So, you know, trustworthiness and discretion are priorities in our—my world."

"Thanks. I appreciate that. It just gets rather lonesome around here some days, and … I appreciate your coming by."

"Not a problem, Warren, but I need to ask you about Trafficanti, too." Max lowered his tone, showing he'd turned serious, too. "I mean, I'm curious. Do you know much about the man? I'd heard … allegations—I guess that's the best word—that he was a mobster, a mafia member, and if you're doing business with him, well, I'd expect there are more reasons …" Max's voice trailed off; he'd noted an abrupt change in the young man's demeanor: his posture had seemed to stiffen.

"There's not a problem!" Warren vehemently protested, his chin raised. "There aren't any conditions! This is just business—I shouldn't have said anything. My father said—" He halted midsentence, mentally searching for what could next be said. "Nothing. Never mind." He appeared to deflate in place.

"Hey, listen," Max comforted, his tone soothing. "Listen. I'm not going to say anything to anyone. I don't have a stake in this. Understand?" He waited until the man nodded. "Now, just to clear the air and get all things said, tell me if I'm right: I'm betting that the distribution trucks are owned by Trafficanti—probably indirectly. And I'm betting the contracts are through the mafia's restaurant connections—hah!" He huffed a quick, cynical laugh. "How'd you like to own one of those restaurants and have the mob set the prices of your supplies? I bet they could limit competition there, too."

Warren grimaced. He failed to see any humor in this observation, but he didn't object. He was again staring vacantly at the greasy floor, making little rainbow arcs with the toe of his rubber boot.

Max continued, "Anyway, I'm guessing your US citizenship and age and background might have influenced you being selected as the person to acquire this business—that and your father's relationship. But, Warren, I'm guessing that there's another shoe still to drop. This is just too good a deal. Someday ... maybe you'll be asked for more money or some kind of assistance in return for this benefit granted you, but you may not know about that now." He looked on as Warren glanced up; their eyes met, and he knew he was correct; he could see the confirmation in the guy's eyes—or, at least, a common suspicion. "OK, so you were told—or it was insinuated, maybe at a meeting with Trafficanti in Tampa—that someday you'd be asked for a favor in return. That right?" He saw the slight nod, and suddenly he didn't want to know anything more. *What good is it doing? Warren's in it already.* He remembered Randal's tax client.

He patted the taller man's shoulder. "Hey, buddy, I should be getting out of your hair. You've probably got a lot of stuff to do.

And, you know, this might not be bad at all. I mean, they need you a lot more than you need them, huh?" He was nodding as he talked. "You've got the clean name and record and can always go back into accounting ... and if the time comes, you can always say no."

Warren raised his eyes; they connected again.

"Well, you know," Max hurried on, "neither of us has been here before, and we've seen a lot of movies—this is just business, and you should treat it like that. I've heard the mob has legitimate businesses, too." He saw a darkening of the other's eyes and wished he'd stopped talking sooner.

• • •

The big door screeched shut, and Max was alone, standing on the loading dock out front and watching the dust settle on his and Warren's cars. A semi had kicked up clouds of the stuff from the road, and it drifted this way with the light fall breeze. *I wish it'd rain.* The city was in the midst of a severe drought, and all lawn sprinkling had been halted. He was thinking about his brown grass when he saw it: the long black car parked across the street. With its deeply tinted windows closed, it looked ominous, menacing, just sitting there. *Even the dust doesn't dare settle in that direction.*

He then noticed the big dude—a Latin-looking fellow in a guayabera shirt—resting against the car, his foot braced on the front bumper, his muscled arms folded across his chest. The guy was silently studying him in return, from his post across the way. Then the man acknowledged him, slowly waving to him without unclasping his arms—barely a hand wave. And a nod.

Now known and identified! Not insignificant any longer! Max double-timed his steps down the concrete stairs toward his car and, after some difficulty with finding and inserting the appropriate key, succeeded in getting his Chevy started and rolling. The man smiled—*smirked*—at him as he roared off. *Should I have covered up my license tag?* That wouldn't have made sense, he decided, or a difference. *I just hope Warren prospers in the olive-oil import trade—for a long, long time.*

. . .

About a year later, almost to the day, Max bumped into Kate Schmotz, Warren's older sister, at a funeral at Congregation Beth. The service had been a hurried affair, as are most Jewish funerals and interments, so they had ample time afterward to saunter along to the parking lot, catching up on each other's lives. They shared a bench in the garden and watched the other attendees jockey for position at the exits. Eventually they got around to business, and Max asked his question: "So how's Warren doing?"

"Well, he's moved … to California. He's out of the olive-oil trade," Kate reported, turning to face him. "He said it was like something you'd told him—that there could be an obligation attached. He said he didn't agree, and a day later, the health-department inspector showed up. He was out of business that same day."

Max puffed his cheeks and stared straight ahead. He didn't ask about the requested favor; he didn't need to know. *And Warren's escaped.* "So how's your dad?" he asked instead.

"I'm suing him," she matter-of-factly replied. "Without my knowledge, he invaded the trust left for me by my grandfather and totally depleted it. You know, I actually paid for that oil business; I just didn't know it at the time."

"Isn't that your father over there? Coming out the side door of the temple?" Max pointed toward the distant figure and stood, as if to go over and greet him.

Kate shook her head and patted his leg. "I wouldn't, if I were you," she warned. "He knows you talked with Warren. He thinks you screwed up his deal and, um, really, really dislikes you. No—more than that—he detests you. So … be careful."

"But—but," Max sputtered, "I didn't tell anyone about that—that situation. Oh, I might have told Randal Minz a few things, but he kept it to himself. He's trustworthy. He wouldn't have said anything."

Kate leaned to one side, looking up from the corners of her eyes. "Minz might have talked to other trustworthy souls, too. Who knows? Bottom line: my father's world crashed around him, and—according to him—someone caused it. Someone snitched to the authorities, and he was put on some kind of blacklist, he believes. And he thinks it was you; he likes thinking it was you; he was told it was you. So he wouldn't welcome any discussions. And, between you and me, Max, he's a sick man—sick both physically and mentally … and probably a dangerous man. You should stay away."

Max looked back toward the building. The distant figure was gone, replaced by a thicker, stronger figure leaning against the wall beside the door. The big man folded his thick arms and gave a small hand wave. *I see you, too.*

CHAPTER 5
EARLY AFTERNOON

"Cole, you think this murder's a mafia job? A hit job?"
Allison's staring at me again, over the tops her spectacles. She's finished reading the second chapter.

"No, no—" I answer. I'm about to say more, but our office door swings open, banging against the stop. One of the techies from Forensics peeks around the corner.

"Got something for me?" I ask. I can't remember the guy's name; he's one of the newer ones down there. I've only talked with him a time or two.

"Detective Eltie?" he asks in return, as if he'd never laid eyes on me before.

"Yes, sir," I answer, keeping my tone neutral. Those guys don't get out much, and, anyway, he's busy ogling Allison. I wait. He's obviously enjoying his visit—and I might need a favor again ... someday. Three, maybe four seconds pass.

"Hey, thanks for the speedy service," I prompt. *That's enough sightseeing for today.* "That the blood work and ballistics stuff on the Anderson case?" I see he has several reports in his hand.

"Eh, yeah—yes, sir." He's looking down at the crisp sheets as if they've just magically appeared in his paws. "Yes, sir," he says again, stepping forward to place them on the corner of my desk. Now he's standing there and studying Allison's legs—I can tell—and she's enjoying the attention, rolling back in her chair and crossing her long limbs at the ankles.

Get a room, you two. "Well, thank you, son," I say. He might stand there for the next hour if I don't refocus his attention on this world: "Anything else ... son?" I put special emphasis on the last word because Detective Bryce is old enough to be his mother.

"Eh, no, sir. Thank you, sir," he stammers, backing out of the room and closing the door behind.

"Older sister," Allison says, guessing my thoughts again. "You're the one old enough to be his father ... sir."

I sniff without replying and reach over to move the lab reports closer so I can read them. I'm careful not to raise my head to focus my bifocals; that'd just give her more ammunition.

"Well, that's interesting," I say, reading the top page. "They say the blood's not a match with Juanita's blood—Juanita Jones."

Allison stops slurping the last of her sweet tea. She'd bought lunch for the two of us. "You fly; I'll buy," she'd said, and I had flown.

"So who's Juanita Jones?" she asks.

I point my pinkie at the pile of papers on her desktop. "You'll need to read the March '83 chapter next. That'll tell you who Juanita Jones is. We've got DNA on her ... and on Howard Fleet—remember him?"

"CFO?" she replies. "Correct?"

"Smart as a whip," I mutter; I've started reading the lab report. "And the blood's not Fleet's either." *Dang!* "I was almost certain it was his." That irritates me; I hate being wrong in my assumptions. I skip to the concluding statement at the bottom and read it aloud: "'However, we believe the submitted evidential material may indicate adulteration; additional testing is in progress.' Well, that figures!" I flip through the remaining pages and toss the reports across the desk to Allison, who has to hurry to catch them before they fall to the floor.

"Whoops! Sorry," I apologize. "Guess I don't know my own strength, huh?"

Allison nails me with one of her frozen-eyed, over-the-top-of-the-specs stares as she deliberately rotates the sheaves on her desk, to read for herself.

The phone rings, and I grab for it, hoping to reverse the sudden atmospheric change in the room. "Eltie," I answer and hear only dead air. I poke the button on a blinking line and try again: "Detective Eltie."

It's Ms. James I hear on the other end. "Ms. Andrea James," she says, as if there were many Ms. James in my world. "Detective Eltie," she continues, "I'm calling from the coroner's offices. This poor man is not my father. I don't know who he is, but he is *not* my father!"

Not Anderson? Dang? Another wrinkle's suddenly appeared in my case, and I realize I've lost a lot of time—and sleep—dealing with false leads ... but I should be happy for her. "He's not?" I manage to croak. "That's ... that's great!"

"Isn't it? See, Daddy's got a tattoo on his upper arm from when he was in the Air Force. He had a computer with wings tattooed on his arm. And this man doesn't have that—the computer with wings!"

"Your father got a box tattooed on his arm?" I'm thinking this guy's about as dull as any other accountant I've known.

"No, no, see? Back in his military days, computers were large with flashing lights, colorful—with tape drives on the front. No wings, but he added them because he was in the US Air Force. I guess you'd have to see it. He was in computer maintenance and was quite proud of his time in the service."

She sounds very lively, very happy—which I'd expect when a loved one has returned from the dead. But now we don't know who the dead guy is or what's happened to Mr. Anderson, do we? So I ask, "Andrea, then do you have an idea as to your father's whereabouts now? I mean, I saw that shotgun and—"

"Oh, that's not my father's shotgun," she interrupts. "That's Mr. Adams's gun. He's the old man who lives next door. He'd seen my father's king snake up in the bird feeder a while back and shot the poor thing into a thousand pieces. On Thanksgiving Day. Dad was so mad he took the gun away and put it in the house. Anyway, Mr. Adams will never miss it; he's a bit senile, you know. And then there was the time ..."

So ol' Max has probably done the world a service what with grabbing the shotgun from a mentally infirm person. But I'm still lost. "Ms. James, Ms. James," I break in, "please help me to understand and to tie up loose ends: Mr. Adams shot the snake and the bird feeder and the house in the process?"

"Nooo." Andrea sounds confused, too. "Mr. Adams didn't shoot the house. He shot in the other direction and almost got the garage—but that's another thing: Daddy's car is gone. I guess he's ... um, maybe he could have told me he was going to be away? Like he could be visiting relatives?—he's done that before, you know." She sounds somewhat meek and apologetic, like this thought just occurred to her. But she recovers quickly and launches into another Daddy story about the time he called her from Alaska after his being away already for a week and a half—a pleasant narrative, I'm sure.

But her thoughts are more pleasant than the ones I'm thinking. Right now, I don't *need* to talk with Ms. James anymore; right now, I don't *want* to talk with Ms. James anymore; I'm frustrated and still thinking about my wasted hours. Trying to keep my voice level, I interrupt again to request that she call their relatives and call me back—later. "Could you do that?" I ask her. I also tell her I'll be out to Mr. Anderson's house later in the afternoon and hang up without saying good-bye. Good-byes with Ms. James, I think, could be rather extensive.

Allison's watching me, having heard my side of the conversation and seeing my complexion redden. "What?" she asks.

"She says the dead guy's not her father." I then summarize what Andrea's just told me. "She says she hasn't a clue as to who the decedent may be. And we certainly don't know who he is."

"So what *were* you thinking?" She leans back in her chair, moving the lab reports to her lap.

I give out a heavy sigh. "Well, first, if that wasn't Mr. Max Anderson laid out on the walkway in front of the house—and it wasn't, according to his daughter—then I'd say a very unlucky Jehovah's Witness chose to visit at the wrong time: when a home invasion was going on. I'd considered that maybe an assailant—or assailants—had decided to invade the home and entered the yard from the back alley when they saw the old man in his bedroom and the car in the garage. They're thinking easy robbery. Or maybe the JW ran into the assailants coming around the house—and got blasted. And Anderson panicked and ran for the woods."

"Not for vengeance or anyone's desire to stop the printing of his tell-all book?"

"Well, no, see, I wasn't initially thinking that—not yet. I mean, who kills accountants over their memoirs?" I chuckle, a brittle sound, even in my own ears. "But that was before I read those chapters. Let me start again."

"Go on."

"So, at first, I'm thinking home invasion with the shotgun and all. That kind of thing has happened before in that neighborhood, with all those old people living there—easy pickings. The assailants, cruising the alley, see Mr. Anderson in the bedroom, enter the yard. and maybe take an accidental shot—chewed-up window frame and wood—and catch a finger, say, in the gun's slide mechanism. That would've accounted for the blood dripped around the side of the house." I see Allison squint with this observation. "It could happen," I insist. "If you put your hand up when the shell's ejected, you can give yourself a pretty good gash right here." I show her the scar on my right hand below my thumb.

"If you say so," she says. "Go on."

I snort my protest. *So impatient.* "OK, OK. See, the gunshot alarms the old man, and he sees the assailant—I'm thinking one person at this time—through the bedroom window. Anderson makes a break for the front door, and the murderer runs around the outside and catches the old man full in the face as he shuffles down the sidewalk. Then the assailant goes in the house, finds the old man's billfold and keys, and hustles out the back door, forgetting the shotgun and leaving it inside the house. Maybe he's worried about the noise or hears sirens."

"OK," Allison says, "that would explain why the victim had no keys in his pocket. But why the tracts?"

I shrug. "Maybe I thought he could have been reading a pamphlet inside the house?"

"And the shells found in the front and back were twelve gauge—not twenty." She's tapping one line on the report with her fingernail. "The shotgun inside the house was probably not the murder weapon either. The pellets were buckshot—in the siding *and* in the deceased." She's grinning at me now.

"Doesn't matter," I sniff. "And the dead guy's not Anderson anyway. And the blood droplets aren't from either Howard Fleet or Juanita Jones. I'm—we're back to square one, and I was wrong."

"Hey, don't get defensive with me. OK? We're just talking still. Where did you get DNA information on Fleet and Jones anyway?"

"Hah! Good question," I say, nodding approvingly. "It seems ol' Max helped put them both in prison—caught them with their hands in their respective cookie jars. Anderson's audit findings—and testimonies afterward—got them both convicted. That's why we got the police records."

"And ..." Allison's expecting more. She knows me.

"And they've both been recently released. So I guess that's what led me in their direction," I admit.

"What about that?" She's pointing at the pistol photo on my desk.

"Well, that's what I was cogitating over this morning—when you came in." I finger the Starbucks coffee cup. It's long been empty, and I've lost track of time. "What say we go find some more coffee and maybe a donut and start again later this afternoon? I've got ballistics and serial-number info still coming ... and prints from off the gas can."

"What gas can?"

"The one they found in the bushes. Right after they found the pistol on the porch roof." My stomach rumbles; I give Allison a sorrowful look.

She shakes her head. "I'll take the March '83 chapter with me to read. You're gonna have more than one donut, aren't you?"

CHAPTER 6
MARCH 1983

Maxwell C. Anderson, certified public accountant and today's driver, began signaling about a half block before the Thirteenth Street intersection, allowing his car to coast the remaining hundred yards or so along Central Avenue as he searched the line of oncoming vehicles, looking for an opening ahead while still keeping tabs on the traffic behind. His eyes nervously flicked to his rearview mirror, then back to the road, and then back again to the mirror. "Eh, Donna, Donna, hang on," he warned aloud, indicating the mirror with a lift of his chin. "Quick left coming, eh, don't think, eh, dude back there, following too close ... maybe can't stop!" He finished in a rush.

Donna M. Goldner, accounting clerk and the only passenger in the car, momentarily twisted about to look behind and make her own assessment—a normal reaction for her—and quickly turned back to brace herself, her hands pressed hard against the Buick's padded dash. "Damn!" she gasped. "Too cloooose!" She closed her eyes and hunched her shoulders, anticipating the almost-certain collision ... and was thumped hard against the door when Max suddenly accelerated, his car's tires squalling through the intersection.

"Whoa!" he breathed; they'd cleared the traffic. "Whoa! Close!" He'd lifted his foot from the gas pedal and now lightly tapped the brakes, continuing to watch behind in the rearview as they slowed. "There he goes," he reported, leaning to his left to follow. "He just drove right on by, that old boy did. On down Central. Old dude ...

aged … him and his old lady." Max huffed another mighty breath. "You know, the old guy was so shrunk up and short—thought for a minute there he was sitting in our backseat. Hah!" he laughed lightly—a cynical sound—and shook his head. "Should've expected it, I guess, when I chose to drive downtown at the noon hour when all these old folks living around here decide to go out to …" He glanced over; Donna was still locked in her head-down, braced-arms position. "…To lunch."

"Uhhh," she moaned to the floor.

"Hey, it's all over now—plenty of room—not even close. You can open your eyes now." He resisted the urge to pat her shoulder. With anyone else, he'd have gone on to joke about their close encounter, but not with Donna. *She'd bite me.* He believed she was about the most humorless person he'd ever known … at least with him. She was so much friendlier with his business partner, Nolan Smith—*but they've known each other a lot longer, too.*

Still tapping and slowing the car, he returned his attention to the road ahead and the next intersection. "So, eh, what were you saying?" he asked, casual-like, even though he knew there had been no ongoing conversation; they'd hardly exchanged a dozen words since leaving the office. *Just say anything … say you're OK. You know you're not injured or anything.* The radio was on, and Culture Club sang softly in the background, "Do you really want to hurt me? Do you really want to make—"

Max grimaced and reached over to a knob on the front panel to click off the sound. "Probably not an appropriate song," he chuckled, "for the circumstances." *Damn! Did it again!* He couldn't help himself; he was trying for "calming" or "reassuring"—not "patronizing" or "flippant." *But she won't see it that way, I bet.* She'd already complained several times to Nolan that he was "always" condescending toward her. *Gosh! Imagine if she's actually bruised something. Worker's comp claim for sure. Maybe a lawsuit for an attack on her life.* He wished he'd waited for a wider opening in the line of traffic. *But that old guy was right on my butt. Regardless …*

He wondered about all the things she could say when they returned to the office: That he was inattentive and reckless? That he was irresponsible? Maybe intentionally so? She had claimed last week that he was constantly looking for ways to make her quit her job, to resign. "Max hates me!" she'd wailed to Nolan behind his closed office door, her raised voice clearly audible through the neighboring wall. *Well, at least she's not saying I propositioned her or something ... not yet anyway. Dang!*

He thought about how long it had been like this, with him being on his guard whenever he was around the girl. This state of constant wariness just wasn't natural—or easy—for him. *Just plain taxing.* And he was never quite sure if his partner would support him—if it came to that. That uncertainty perhaps bothered him even more than anything Donna could do.

So why did I ask her to come with me today? He was usually able to minimize his contact with her. *Oh yeah.* Then he remembered: Nolan was supposed to have come with him—them. He was supposed to have accompanied them to meet with the new client but had begged off at the last minute, saying, "I'll meet Lin and his staff another time, Max. I've had an emergency come up. Besides, Cooper's Electronics is your client—you brought 'em—and Donna should ride along with you. She needs to be there if just to be introduced to their bookkeeper ... since she'll be doing their monthly write-up work. Right? That's to be her job. Right?" *Trapped.*

Max glanced over again. Donna had turned in her seat and was staring intently at him, her head cocked to one side, her face radiating an emotion he couldn't immediately decipher, one that was directed either at the moment or at him—and was still ripening behind her squinting eyes. *Dang! What's she thinking now?*

He almost killed me, and he's rattling on about a song? she marveled to herself, enjoying the rising heat of her indignation—righteous indignation. *What an asshole!* She saw him smile again—a wider, toothier version this time—and the heat increased. *A goddamn silly asshole, too!* Straightening in her seat, she released her own puffed-cheeked exhalation, sounding more of impatience, or maybe disgust, than of relief. "Yes," she replied, her voice low and controlled. "I believe that song is appropriate. Entirely appropriate." Another breath. "You know, sometimes I think you're … you're …" Then she abruptly turned away, tight jawed and shaking her head, to glare fiercely out the side window at the passing scene. Several seconds passed. "Never mind," she finally snarled.

More time passed as she arranged and filed her hot thoughts.

"And you know what?" she resumed, now articulating her words through clenched teeth. "They should not be allowing old farts, like those old farts sitting over there, to either own cars or to drive on the roads … either." If Max had caught the emphasis on the latter *either*, he chose not to reply. And the old farts along the sidewalk continued to stare back at them from their green-painted perches. "Just look at them sitting there," she growled. "Row after row of benches. Look at them. Just sitting there and watching the cars drive by. Doing nothing but just sitting! Insipid!" Clipped words repressing anger.

Feeling a certain gratitude toward those bench-sitters, Max did as she asked and looked: along the way here, on Thirteenth Street, he noticed, the benches were actually spaced farther apart than those to the east, along Central Avenue and closer to the downtown area, but were just as densely occupied at this time of day. And now, judging from the appreciative grins on the faces of the elderly spectators, still nudging one another and pointing, he guessed that the location had been carefully chosen over those benches fronting the intersections to the east, those intersections with new signal lights and safer left-turn lanes. *Bless your ancient hearts.*

"Damn green benches," Donna spat, concluding her dark observations.

"Made Saint Petersburg famous at one time, you know," Max helpfully noted. *Now why did you say that? You could have gone all day—*

Her anger flared anew. "Yeah. Yeah, but when people get so old they can't drive, they shouldn't … it's getting so I hate to come downtown when ..." Her voice trailed off. *Doesn't matter. Why bother? Asshole.* She puffed her cheeks, allowing the air to slowly escape. Nolan had told her she should work on curbing her emotions and "checking the negative stuff"—her attitude—until she'd calmed down and examined alternatives. "Choose your words with more discretion," he'd said. "Be professional." *But I'm just too damn honest,* she reasoned.

• • •

Max had arrived in her world last year, joining Nolan Smith in a partnership arrangement that Donna had secretly hoped would one day be hers. She had started working for the accounting practice *(Nolan's accounting practice)* directly out of college and had happily labored for him *(with him)* for over four years now, developing the expectation that, someday, when she'd finally passed the CPA exam, she would become his partner. *Just us.* That was another thing: As the years had passed, and after many long, late hours *(together)*, this secret hope had grown and matured in her heart until one day it occurred to her that maybe she wanted more than just a business partnership with Nolan. *Maybe a relationship with real security?*

She'd already been married, once, early, just out of high school, to an immature man of minimal means, she'd discovered, and below-average aspirations—her characterization—who fled the marriage in its first year. "Just as well," she'd consoled herself at the time. "He'll never amount to anything anyway." And while she had come to regard her ex-husband as being generally inadequate, especially in the areas of ambition and intellect *(barely enough to leave town to avoid paying alimony)*, she'd never doubted her own store of those qualities—for her future. Perhaps she'd not wanted a passenger along on her road to success anyway? So, with student loans providing the funding, she chose to matriculate in the community college, graduated with a degree in accounting, and scored a promising position with the newly formed company, Nolan Smith, CPA, PA. Donna Goldner was indeed smart and ambitious ... and motivated.

· · ·

When Nolan had interviewed and hired her, he'd said she was a "go-getter," having the kinds of qualities he was seeking in building his staff; at their initial interview, he offered her the job. He seemed to have recognized in her the same something that had caused him to initially go out on his own, to build his own practice apart from the other CPA firms in town. Plus, he noticed, she was a very attractive lady. With her drive and abilities—*and looks*, he admitted to himself—he imagined her to be the ideal type of employee he would need to grow his company: independent and proficient with a great grade point average, perhaps sought after by the other accounting firms, with the potential to draw clients from all across town—maybe from all across the state.

"Appearances really are very important in business, you know," he'd once told his wife, Valarie. He had been in the profession for many years, having joined with one of the big eight accounting practices early on when his first employer had been acquired and merged into the larger firm. And at Ander & Co., he'd been immediately impressed *with* and intensely schooled *in* the qualities they expected of their CPA staff: conservative attire (dark suits, white shirts, solid ties, and narrow-brimmed hats for outside wear—it *was* the sixties), appropriate personal deportment (reserved, studious, and obedient), and slender young bodies with single marital statuses. However, because Nolan had satisfied neither of these latter two qualities, it was propitious that his former employer had been bought by Ander & Co.; otherwise, he might never have been hired. And though he'd seldom mulled over fairness and equality in his workplace, he'd known how it was to be: the bright and beautiful always broke early to the lead, ahead of the diligent plodders.

But he was a plodder. Of course, he would never have labeled himself as such, if he even allowed himself to think further along in that direction. He'd most certainly never revealed such concerns to anyone in the firm—that his appearance label was a major factor in his being passed over for partnership those many times during his Ander & Co. years. Yet he'd been inwardly influenced by the company's culture: predisposed to favor those types of people, the attractive people, when given a choice in the firm's personnel additions. The proof was hanging on his office wall: pictures of his various teams' moments, row after row of smiling young men and women—well-suited, fetching, and comely—and Nolan Smith, their manager, standing in the pictures' backgrounds, balding and overweight.

The next principle he'd have espoused, if he'd thought more about it: neither brightness nor beauty guaranteed the early leaders more than a moment at the front of the rat race; the diligent plodders—even the short, fat plodders—could and did excel through hard work, perseverance, and "soft skills." He was his own best attestation of that fact, having had some of the firm's most valued clients follow after him when he'd gone out on his own. He possessed those technical skills his clients sought; he was competent and could do their work; and he had the soft skills that had motivated them to want to continue to work with him, to plan with him, to feel confidence in his regard for their businesses. Soft skills meant honesty, respect, decency, and more: they're associated with people and interactions, the ability to understand others and to effectively communicate with them. But as he was soon to realize, those skills had somehow failed to flourish in the character of his new accounting hire, Donna M. Goldner.

His clients had called him after hours, requesting confidentiality as well as the reassignment of their work to other accountants, usually telling him of her rudeness, her abruptness, her impatience; they'd said they "couldn't work with her." Nolan's two other staff members had simply asked for physical separation from her, an easier accommodation since accounting is a solitary occupation.

Yet he had not fired her.

In dealing with the complaints, Nolan had acknowledged to several close clients that perhaps *he* was at fault; that he'd hired too quickly for the demands of the position; that, in favoring certain attributes, he'd failed to look much beyond her GPA for clues that she would have difficulty in working with others. He hadn't pressed for references with her résumé or requested recommendations from former employers and coworkers—procedures normally carried out by clerks at Ander & Co. In short, he'd assumed personal responsibility for her failures. "Accordingly," he had told Valarie, "I should make the best of the situation for the both of us," and he vowed to "mentor her to success"—his second error in judgment. He'd believed he could teach those necessary personal skills, those soft skills. After all, she was beautiful.

A full year had passed, and then another and another, and the firm had not thrived as Nolan had expected; he'd maintained essentially the same clientele and staff level he'd had three years prior. His subsequent personnel additions had not remained long after their hire, and Donna remained unable to form close connections with the majority of his clients. As a result, Nolan had dithered in fully turning over the clients' monthly accounting responsibilities to her, the job she'd been hire to do, justifying the delays to himself—and her—as being "exceedingly complex client situations" or "excessively steep learning curves." Thus, he couldn't grow; he didn't have time to market his firm; he was too busy fronting for her, doing much of the detailed work that she should have been doing.

Still, he would not consider firing her, for, as he'd *not* shared with Valarie, he had come to … *really like her.* She made him feel special in a way he'd never felt before, flirting with him, bringing him his morning coffee and newspaper, showing him she really liked him, too, the fat boy, the plodder. So he'd doubled down, resolving to continue to work with her, to develop her professional skills, to "smooth her edges," to teach her to sublimate those reported-to-him traits of hostility while somehow managing to keep her in separate office space. "She's feeling so much anger," he'd told his wife, "probably from being rejected when she was young and feeling inferior." He himself could certainly understand how another person could have such feelings (though, in truth, Donna had not felt inferior a day in her life but never felt the need to tell him otherwise). Besides, he'd reasoned, his spouse had a well-paying job; the financial bottom line of his practice wasn't crucial to their livelihood ... until that day, about a year ago, when Valarie had said it was. That had been the day he'd returned Max's phone call, scheduling a time for them to meet to discuss the combining of their practices.

• • •

About that same time, when Nolan and Max were discussing their joint futures, Donna had concluded that her boss's marriage was the primary obstacle in her road to success, *her* future. *Strategy.* While she'd believed the two of them—she and Nolan—shared deep and growing feelings of affection, she had also determined that she would have to make the first move. She'd interpreted his failures to act on her overtures as his charming shyness, or naïveté, rather than as any reluctance to have sex with her, or as any kind of special faithfulness to his wife. In fact, she'd recalled, during several of their frequent lunches together, he had shared his very personal stories with her—of his growing-up years, his overly religious and restrictive family background, his poor self-image as a fat child, and his total lack of dating experiences prior to his marriage. He had even once confided to her, in whispered trust, that he had been a virgin on his wedding night. *Telling me that secret meant trust ... and love ... didn't it?* So when she'd hinted at a closer relationship and found him to be rather unresponsive, she thought him to be sexually unschooled rather than unwilling. After all, she had never, ever been spurned by a man—not since she was fourteen and had started growing amazing breasts.

Having determined her need for action, she'd set about implementing her plan: on that day, she'd selected her lowest-cut knit top, a revealing number that would usually cause Nolan to stutter and lose his place when she would lean across his desk, and arrived early at the office to make coffee *just the way he likes* after having stopped on the way in to buy a dozen Krispy Kreme donuts—also *because he really likes them*. Then, when she'd heard him arrive, she had dashed to the breakroom, poured his coffee, and selected a favorite jelly donut, carrying both around to his office. *Special delivery.*

They had talked for several minutes about the day's assignments, and when she'd judged the timing optimal (Nolan having lost his struggle to keep his eyes lowered and his concentration on the workpapers spread across his desk), she'd slipped around to stand beside him, ostensibly to view a column of figures from the same side, and leaned forward so her right arm lay across his shoulders, her dark tresses lightly brushed the side of his neck, and her mostly bare breasts jiggled just inches from his flushed cheek. Silence. Then she had slowly, tenderly, eased him back from his desk with her right hand and cupped his broad chin with her left, raising his lips to her own.

The explosion had been immediate: he'd pushed away from his desk, crashing his chair into the credenza behind while barely missing her toes in his retreat. "Donna!" he'd blurted, standing plastered against the far wall. "I'm married, and this—this isn't right!" Nolan had managed again to display the moral convictions that had once caused a client, an Episcopal minister, to label him as the most ethical heathen he'd ever known. (Nolan actually leaned to the agnostic point of view.)

In the following days, as their mutual embarrassments had eased, they'd more or less reconciled and returned to their former state—or Nolan's believed former state—of boss/mentor and employee. But Donna still held fast her hopes of eventual partnership, even after that later spring day when Nolan brought Max into the office and informed her that the two of *them*, Max and Nolan, had decided to combine clientele, libraries, equipment—and personnel. She would be expected to work for this interloper … too.

More days and weeks passed, and she had stayed on, persevering but never forgetting her eventual goals and never completely laying aside her resentment of the new guy, as Max would remain to her. And only occasionally would her covert attacks be detected—those efforts to sabotage the budding partnership: her differing treatment of clients, Nolan's and Max's; her selective remembering of instructions, Nolan's and Max's; her frequent failures in forwarding messages, mainly Max's; and so on. But she'd seldom failed in sharing criticisms and disparaging remarks about the new guy with the clients and other staff members when given the opportunity.

• • •

This morning, Nolan had taken a detour to her office when he arrived to tell her that something had come up and he would be unable to accompany them to Cooper's Electronics. He'd gone on to say this new client had a great reputation and was a most desirable addition to their practice and she would be "well-advised" to start fresh with their officers and personnel. The money from this client, he'd said, could make a big difference in the firm's future employment decisions. Nolan had intended to clearly communicate to her that his partner was no longer agreeable to providing the extensive write-up services he'd accepted over the past year and that they'd agreed to employ another accountant, if only to support Max's clients.

But Donna had heard "…this client was good for big fees" and "…definitely one to be retained." She'd understood *she* was appointed to do the write-up work and that *she* needed to be in the client's business starting from day one to review the accounting systems and procedures for *herself*—and not to rely on Max for information. She was to walk through the recordings of sales, trace the postings of invoices, witness the punching of time cards, and so on—to make the client reliant on her and to make Max superfluous to them. *Now this was a plan!*

Meanwhile, Nolan had left her office this morning thinking about how well she'd taken the news. It had been hard for him to tell her that his days as her mentor were drawing to a close, that he was advising her to step up now and take responsibility … and that he would no longer interface with clients for her. Today was his first step. *I don't have a choice.*

Because, the previous evening, he had met with Max to talk about the general direction of their business and the accounting demands of taking on a new and probably very dependent client and had been confronted with … *an honest man's perception of my relationship with Donna.* He'd been made to recognize his emotional attachment to the woman for what it was—and continued to be. For, in talking with his partner, he'd been gripped with shame when Max had quietly inquired, "Is, um, Donna maybe a really good friend of yours or something? I mean I can understand loyalty and nepotism but …" While the man had not finished his sentence and had asked in probably the most tactful manner he could've managed, he'd most succinctly communicated his impressions and probably those of the remainder of the staff. *An affair! Something exceeding an employee relationship! Valarie! Had she seen, too?*

Afterward, he'd gone home and been unable to sleep, continuing to ruminate over the stormy exchange that had followed—composed primarily of his enthusiastic justifications and denials *(way too enthusiastic).* Lying there in bed, staring at the ceiling, he'd thought past the perceived questioning of his morals and the extreme umbrage he'd taken at the time to consider—and appreciate—the actual limits of his partner's inquiry: *it had been just business to him; Max wasn't judging or accusing me.*

Hours later, propped up in the recliner in his study, he'd concluded his mulling: *Max is a better manager than me.* "After all, I'm the one who hasn't been performing the job I'm supposed to do. I caused harm to the firm and the futures of those people who've committed to it … and perhaps to my marriage. In doing the work someone else should have been doing, I've ignored my own responsibilities. I've been uneven with the other staff members, dishonest with them … and with my wife. I owe them all … taken Donna's side far too many times with the staff and the clients … defended her, asking them to try to see things from her position, to be more considerate of her feelings. …"

So, first thing this morning, he'd laid it out to Donna: she'd better be able to get along with and to maintain a professional attitude with this client, or they would have to find another person to do the job. *Actions have consequences. But maybe I should actually have said she'd be fired? Ah well.*

· · ·

That's probably why Max is Nolan's partner and I'm not, Donna determined. "I'm just too damn honest!"

"So you don't like … what?" Max asked. "I didn't hear what you said." He'd stopped the car before the intersection on First Avenue North and leaned far forward in his seat, searching past her for traffic coming toward them along the broad four-lane street, traveling one way, east to west, right to left. "I thought you were talking about … maybe something happening here."

"Damn! It sure takes you a while to process stuff!" she blurted, whirling about to face him. "Here we were almost killed, and you're thinking of something I never said … never mind. We weren't talking. OK? Just … never mind."

"Look … I'm sorry?" he halfway apologized. "Now, if you wouldn't mind sitting back, I can't see past you." He was making extra sure this time there was a long, long break in the oncoming line of traffic before he chanced a crossing.

She folded her arms across her chest and huffily pushed back in her seat. "OK now? OK?" *He's trying to look down my dress, I bet.*

"Yeah. Thanks." He eased the big Buick forward as the last of the westbound mass of automobiles cleared the intersection. In the next block, he signaled and veered into the vacant lot off to the right, through a break in the granite curbing, onto a sandy two-lane path that wound through the weeds to a flat crushed-shell area bordering the asphalt parking area ahead.

"Can't even feel the bumps here, can you? Or even back there on the street, on the brick surface, can you?" Max patted the car's oversized steering wheel. "1956 Buick Special. They don't make 'em like this anymore, do they? I mean, if that old man's Falcon *had* hit us … um, never mind."

He halted the car at the far end of the long array of vehicles edging the asphalt. "Lin likes to leave the spaces on the pavement for customers," he explained, pushing the shifter to park and then, out of habit, setting the foot brake. "Business looks brisk today, doesn't it?" Only two or three spaces remained open on the paved surface, the others being evenly occupied by commercial and private vehicles. "Cooper's sells to electronic vendors and the general public both," he explained. "That's why there are so many business trucks and vans in the parking lot."

"While we have to walk through palmettos and sandspurs," Donna groused.

"What?" He clicked the ignition switch to the off position—he rarely used a key to start his car—and the Buick instantly quieted. "Saying something about … what? I couldn't hear you."

"Nothing," she snapped, pulling at her door handle. "Just forget it. Let's go!" They opened their doors in unison.

At the car's front bumper, Max hesitated, almost waiting for her while she retrieved her calculator case from off the back floor, before striding on to the building. Normally he'd have raced around to open the door for a lady and would have offered to carry her cases—*but not for Donna.* She'd more than once snatched away her burden, refusing to allow him to assist her in any way, not deigning to allow the most common of courtesies. "Sexist ingratiation," she'd claimed. *And all right by me,* he thought. *Just the same* ... He figured her calculator case and audit bag must weigh at least thirty pounds combined.

Reaching the entrance of the windowless two-story building, he grasped the right-side handle and swung wide the heavy solid-core wooden door ... and stepped through, leaving the panting, sweating girl trudging far behind on the superheated sidewalk. He counted to ten as he stood there, just inside the door, and then backed against it, pushing it wide. "Madam, may I offer some assistance?" he asked, wide-eyed and innocent.

She didn't reply, but her hot eyes said, "Screw you!" She huffed past him and into the store's cool, tastefully dim interior.

"So, Donna, have you been here before?" Max pleasantly asked, as he waved to the suited and vested salesman standing behind the glass counter in the pool of light straight ahead.

"No," she answered, easing her cases to the thick carpet. "So where's the office? Where's their bookkeeper?" *Where's the friggin' water fountain, you ass!*

"All in good time. Let me first introduce you to Mr. Nathan Dawson." He raised his voice on the latter words and waved again at the tall blond man.

"I don't need to meet some friggin' salesclerk," she growled.

Max grimaced. "Maybe this isn't such a good idea after all, Donna. When Nolan called this morning and said ... You know, maybe it'd be better if we come back later ... when he's able to come with us. Meantime, while you go back to the car, I'll check with Ms. Jones to see if—"

"OK, OK," Donna interrupted. "Hey, I'm sorry. OK? I'm over-heated. I just need some water." *I need this client.* "Suppose we start again—yes, I would dearly love to meet Mr. Nate Dawson."

"Nathan. His name is Nathan. He doesn't like being called Nate."

"OK then. Nathan. Good Lord! Whatever!"

"Donna—" Max was watching the salesman, still standing behind his counter some twenty feet away. *Gosh, I hope he can't hear us.*

"OK! OK! Sorry again." She turned and smiled sweetly at Nathan, nodding to him. "Let's go meet Mr. Dawson." She bent to pick up her cases and marched on toward the sales counter, straightening her back as she walked to accentuate her bust. *These boobs are for you, Nate-boy.*

Nathan smiled again, coming from behind his counter and circling around to meet her halfway, capping his fountain pen as he walked.

Montblanc. She recognized his expensive pen's chunky shape, and her smile broadened. She lowered her cases to the carpet and extended a limp hand, allowing him to walk the remainder of the way to her. "Nathan. Nathan. So good to finally meet you," she gushed, turning slightly to give him a profile view of cleavage. "Max has told me all about you." *Handsome, too.* She evaluated him as he walked: *razor-cut hairstyle, about six two in a tailored three-piece suit, well-shined wingtip oxfords.*

He took her offered hand in his own and leaned close, almost as in a bow, almost as if he intended to kiss her hand.

Whoa! She felt instant heat in her nether regions.

"And you must be Ms. Goldner," he greeted in return, his voice low and warm, without any perceptible accent. "Miss Donna Goldner?"

"Eh … yes." *Oh damn! Blue, blue eyes. French accent, too!*

One beat and then two. Their eyes met, and a long second passed—a meaningful second to her—before he reluctantly released her digits and turned to Max, to grip the other's extended paw while loudly patting his biceps with a free hand—heartily, man-style. "And where is Mr. Nolan Smith today, Mr. Anderson?" he asked, again displaying his dazzling dental work.

This guy is good, Max noted. After melting the elastic in Donna's shorts, Nathan had given him the comradely side-of-the-arm slap and not the domineering top-of-the-shoulder massage. *No wonder he's their top salesman and manager.* "Good afternoon to you, too, Nathan," he heartedly replied, acknowledging the greeting. "Mr. Smith? Well, see, we got problems back at the fort today, and Nolan couldn't come with us—a last-minute thing—a client problem. You know how that goes." They again exchanged nods and smiles, bonding.

"So how are you and Lin doing today?" Max continued. "And how's Miss Jones doing? Anything I should know since our planning meeting last week? You remember?"

During that meeting, Nathan had voiced an expectation—and concern—that their bookkeeper would be resistant to any accounting changes in the store. "Extremely resistant," he'd said. Now he hesitated, glancing over his shoulder before answering, his voice lowered: "Well, Max, Miss Juanita is not any too happy with your coming, you know." He checked again to his rear. "She's really, really upset that you're replacing Mr. Green and has been after Lin all morning … since she was informed of the impending changes."

"Ooo, thanks. I'll avoid handshakes with her then. How about you? What do you think about changing accountants? Good? Bad? Indifferent?"

"Me? Oh, I think it's great. I voted for the resolution at our board meeting." Last year, Nathan had been rewarded with gifted shares and a seat on the company's board of directors. "Leonard Green is getting some age on him, and, frankly, I've been some-what concerned about some of the financial statement presenta-tions and bookkeeping practices—but then I'm not an accountant either."

Max laughed. "Yeah, I hear you, Mr. Modest. I bet you know a lot about how things work around here finance-wise and have lots of suggestions. We'll talk more later. OK? But for now, with Juanita Jones—she is in today, isn't she? I'd like to introduce my accounting associate to her." He glanced over at Donna. "Our accountant who will be responsible for working with her." *Nolan said last night he'd be clear when he talked with her this morning.*

Nathan shifted his attention back to Donna and retrieved the hand she'd not yet lowered. "Then, please, do not leave this lovely one alone with Juanita. It'd be a shame if—"

"Juanita talked hard to her?" Max interrupted, chuckling. "Yeah, that'd be a problem all right. Donna's probably never heard … umm." He'd just caught her stony glare, served up when Nathan had looked aside, away from her to him; he had no difficulty whatsoever in interpreting her unspoken threat. *Most humorless person I've ever known.* For a moment there, he'd almost forgotten.

"Eh, Nathan," he continued smoothly, "maybe you should personally give the young lady an overview of Cooper's Electronics … while I talk with Lin. I'm sure she'd appreciate an intimate presentation of the sound systems you sell and the services you provide."

Nathan rotated back to Donna, whose glower had magically vanished, replaced by a sparkling smile. "Great idea," he agreed, moving his hand to the small of her back, easing her toward the closest showroom—all without encountering the least resistance. "But then you may have to come find us when you're ready for her." He leered at Donna, and her smile broadened.

Best salesman I've ever seen. Max watched them stroll away, disappearing into the McIntosh showroom, before turning and striding away himself. *Bet she'll let him open the door for her. And I bet she's never seen a $20,000 stereo system before either.* He knew he'd have lots of time to talk with Lin.

Angling toward the elevated, half-glassed-in office space at the far corner of the showroom, he passed several very long, very full rows of gondola shelving. He knew this was where Lin had, at one time, earned the majority of his sales: commercial electronics parts and supplies. However, with the introduction of solid-state circuitry, printed-circuit cards, and integrated chips, together with the resultant improvements in component reliability, all at a reduced cost, the need for electronic parts—vacuum tubes, resistors, capacitors, and even transistors—was shrinking, along with the jobs for the people who would have repaired TVs and radios using these parts. He paused to watch the men in the aisles, reading specifications on the backs of boxes and thumbing through the parts catalogs hanging from the shelves. *Soon these guys will be ... what? Fixing computers? Swapping out circuit boards?* He picked up his pace; the thought had somehow depressed him.

"Whatcha got there, old man?" Max called out, taking the office steps in two strides. He'd seen the top of Lin's balding head bobbing above the half doorway as he worked at the keyboard of his newest acquisition, an IBM PC AT.

"Hey, boy," Lin replied, looking up and pushing his glasses onto his forehead. "Come in, come in. Take a seat. Close the door behind you."

Max eased shut the door, listening for the click of the latch. "There."

He selected the wheeled chair in front of the cluttered desk, rolling it over beside the stool where Lin was seated at the computer console. "Whatcha got there?" he again asked.

Lin beamed his reply; he was obviously very proud of his still-new acquisition. His pale-blue eyes danced with excitement and intelligence.

Max was instantly reminded of his childhood and the elf who had always been pictured on the Co-op calendar's December page—a tiny sprite who reliably assisted Santa in the filling of his Christmas sleigh. Like Lin, the elf was small, quick, and cunning, and his head was topped with snow-white hair that thinned to fuzz at the crown. And—unlike Santa—both Lin and the elf possessed ruddy, beardless cheeks that had probably changed little from the time they were born: baby faces—chubby, pink, and always ready for the next giggle.

"It's my newest toy, kiddo," Lin appropriately stated, "the one you're going to help make pay for itself. But I guess I've had it for a while now—so not so new. Watch this." He tapped the enter key, and the screen flicked to an index.

Max leaned in to read the white type on the orange field: "General ledger, sales, and A/R, A/P ... say, nice package. Where'd you get it?"

"Came with the machine. It's got two hundred fifty-six kilobytes of RAM, dual five-and-a-quarter floppy drives, a PC DOS operating system ..." Lin continued on for another two minutes, extolling the power and capacity of his state-of-the-art IBM computer, with frequent comparisons drawn to an earlier and probably inferior model, the IBM PC XT—the exact model Nolan and Max had acquired for their accounting practice just months before.

As he listened to Lin, Max recognized a few of the terms, words familiar to him from having worked with their own office computer. However, it was also clear to him the old man knew far more about the inner workings of the machine than about the uses of the application program running on the machine. He'd have to ask again: "So whatcha got on it now? Whatcha using it for already?"

"Well ... I've got the inventory on it ... completely. I've inputted that already."

"*You* inputted it?" Max asked. He leaned back in his chair, looking about as if searching for someone.

"Yeah, I understand what you're saying. See, Juanita's still having a tough time just learning to navigate around."

"What about Mr. Green?" Max persisted. "Has Leonard been working with it? What accounting-type functions does he already have on it?"

Lin frowned and looked slightly pained, and Max knew why: he'd once visited Leonard Green at his jumbled in-home office to purportedly "interview" him, an Introduction to Accounting class assignment designed to wet the feet of aspiring accountants with early exposure to career realities, as recounted by involved practitioners. And while he had known Mr. Green to be a nice man, gracious in allowing himself to be interviewed for the school project, it was soon apparent the aged fellow had learned his accounting craft perhaps decades before and failed to keep up with changes in the profession over the intervening years. Several times during the interview, Max had to explain now-basic accounting terminology and principles before Mr. Green could respond to his queries.

As it was, the paper had turned out to be exceedingly brief—and gracious.

"Say, how old is Leonard anyway?" Max asked, not waiting for answers to his earlier questions. He guessed Lin probably didn't know what accounting functions were being used by the other man anyway or what was available in the package. He'd have to do some reading and researching on his own.

"Well, over twenty-one, I'm sure. And you got here a lot earlier than I expected, young man." Lin had, in turn, guessed Max had likewise divined his deficiency of accounting knowledge; he pointed to the row of manuals stacked neatly in the bookshelf beside the table. "I was just about to open … volume two."

"Volume one deals with inventory accounting?"

"Yep," the old man laughed. "I was trying to get Juanita up to speed—she's learned to enter sales information from off the invoices, but she seems to be having difficulty with the recording of sales and the removal of the inventory items sold. Know what I mean? But we're still keeping the books the old way, too."

Max nodded his understanding.

"And, see, we've always had problems with getting the sales journals to reconcile to the general ledger cash numbers—Mr. Green has to wrestle with that each week—so I guess, in trying to adjust inventory numbers with sales invoices, well, we should have expected stops and starts."

Max sat upright in his chair; he'd caught a hint of serious concern in Lin's words—and that concerned him. His auditor senses tingled and awakened. "Could you tell me a bit more about that?"

"Well, you know, the cash-register tapes don't always—well, see, the tapes seldom equal exactly what's deposited in the bank. It's just, you know—it's just close. But you know how sales guys are—"

"What's Leonard Green say about it?"

"He says it's close, and when you consider the whole month and … well, you know how Juanita frightens him. I think he's afraid to sit down with her. I think he's afraid to spend much time with her to reason out why there are differences and to figure out what must be done to make things easier to reconcile. That's actually one of the reasons I called you."

"She's unpleasant with him?"

Lin chortled. "Yeah. Saying she's unpleasant is putting it mildly. But then she's unpleasant with everybody, Max. She's very smart, and she's kept the store's books for almost twenty years now, even back when my father—she knows this stuff backward and forward so—"

"Is Juanita especially close to you, Lin? Maybe a personal friend or something?"

The old man's head jerked about; he fixed Max with a long, intense stare. "You mean like is she a girlfriend to me?"

Wow! That wasn't the meaning Max had intended; he was surprised Lin had so quickly jumped to that conclusion—much like the way Nolan had done the previous evening. *Must be the way I'm saying stuff.* "No, no, I didn't mean that. Jeez, at your age ... and the fact that Dorothy would whack off your—"

"Hah!" Lin laughed. "She would at that, son. Me and the ol' woman have been married fifty-two years now, and she still terrifies me. No, I understand what you're saying; I'm just having some fun with you. You're asking if I give Juanita more slack than I would any other employee, if I expect less of her than I would anyone else. And I probably do because I know less about her job, accounting rules and such, than any other position in the store. I know electronic parts and televisions and stereos and such, but I don't hardly know debits and credits ... and they bore me to death."

"Accuracy isn't asking too much, you know," Max quietly observed.

"Yeah, yeah, I know. But it always seems to come with additional costs that make total accuracy completely impractical. Sometimes close is good enough for an engineer. No, I understand what you're saying, and I ... Juanita has been very close to me and my family for many years. She comes to our house on Thanksgiving—several of the staff do—and she's always buying gifts for my boys and Dorothy. You know, she really doesn't have to work; she's independently wealthy. She once told me she inherited a lot of money from her grandfather. Jones of New York. You've heard of them, haven't you?"

"Yes, I think so. They make clothing for women, I believe—not that I'd know anything about that, of course."

"Hah!" Lin snorted. "You mean accountants like to dress up every now and again? Just want to look pretty sometimes?"

This banter was an old joke between them. When he and his wife had first met Max, and Dorothy had discovered the young man to be single, she'd immediately tried to pair him with her brother Joel's oldest daughter. When he'd demurred, citing existing entanglements, Dorothy had somehow understood that to mean he was gay. She'd confided to her husband later that evening that perhaps they should instead introduce Max to Nathan, another nice man who worked at the store. "They might get right along quite well," she'd said. Lin had not corrected her conclusion, thinking it all most amusing, and had instead shared her comments with Max and Nathan at the first opportunity. Nathan, in turn, had thought Dorothy's comments were hilarious and said so "because Max is definitely not gay," while Max had been less amused; he'd been distracted by Nathan's statement, thinking, *So Nathan is? Dang! He's about the most studly guy I know.* And neither of the men had ever corrected Dorothy for essentially mirror-opposite reasons: "Damn! Maybe she'll be a great referral source," and "Damn! Maybe she'll stop trying to hook me up now." Nathan was much less private about sexual matters than Max.

"Well, it never hurts, I guess," Max smiled and nodded; he was no longer so entangled. "Even accountants sometimes want to look pretty. Back to Juanita: does she seem especially wealthy? I mean, other than her saying so, how do you know she's rich? And what does that do for you? Do you, by chance, trust her more? Is that why you don't worry about—you said the deposits don't exactly tie to the daily cash-register tapes, the Z-Outs?"

Lin absently stroked his baby-smooth chin. "Eh, yeah, the Z-Out ... it doesn't always agree with the bank deposit. But it's close over a weekly period of time, you know. And I guess I haven't worried much about, you know, theft because she never seems to be in need of money. Man, you should have seen some of the nice gifts Juanita gave the boys at Christmastime! And last Christmas she gave Dorothy a really nice watch. She drives a late-model Mercedes. She lives in one of those expensive high-rise apartments facing Tampa Bay. No, no, she has way too much money to be concerned with ... stealing—that word's hard to get out." He shook his head. "And, see, our little place doesn't generate that much money anyway. Never has."

It was now Max's time to ponder. He sighed deeply several times and then stood and pointed to the doors along the back wall. "Well, we'll see, I guess. Say, is one of those Miss Jones's office? Or is that hers?" He pointed at the cluttered desk. "And where is she right now?"

The old man pulled at his chin. "Well, I—I don't know. I told her you'd be coming in after lunch—she's been really mad at me all morning—so she said she wanted to get a bite to eat before you got here; she left about thirty or so minutes ago. And, I guess, neither one of us really expected you to arrive this early; traffic can be really bad around here at noon, you know."

Max smiled. "Yeah, I *do* know ... and you aren't the only one with someone mad at you. So where's her office?"

Lin pursed his lips, frowning as he answered, "Well, it's like this. Juanita has two desks. One back there to the right and this desk here. She keeps her inventory and computer records here—packing slips, purchase journal, that kind of stuff—and the sales and banking information back there. She makes a daily deposit at the bank, you know, and the slips are back there in her desk. And Leonard works over there when he comes in every week—right next to her office."

He pointed at an open doorway. "She says she likes him close there so she can quickly answer his questions—and get him out of here. He's distracting, she says. And smells. She says he smells bad, like he doesn't bath often enough, so she wants him in and out." He shrugged slightly. "I can understand that."

"Does he? Stink I mean."

"Well, I've never tried to kiss him or anything," he said, grinning mischievously. "Never pulled his finger, either."

Max grinned back. "Gosh, you're as bad as me, with cracks like those. Has Mr. Green … does Mr. Green seem to have a sweet, medicinal odor like he's sick or something? You know, diabetes can—"

"No, no. That was just Juanita saying that. Me? I've never noticed a smell of any kind. I doubt I would. Dorothy says I'm the most unobservant man she's ever known."

"Hah!" Max laughed. "You're looking at the second-most unobservant man right here. Oh, wait." He'd spotted the top of Nathan's well-coiffed head moving along behind the Sony gondola near the entrance. "Let me go talk with my associate over there—Ms. Donna Goldner for your information *(Lin's terrible with remembering names)*—and we'll get started. I'll ask Nathan to X-Out the cash register to get a subtotal for the day so Donna can see the way the paper tape looks; I'll show her how to tie the tape to the cash deposit for the day." He glanced around again. "And if you're OK with it, I'll let her set up back there in Leonard's office and review files and such in there with him … when he gets here. He *did* say he was coming in today, didn't he?" That had been the principal reason for Donna's coming with him today. *Be a shame if …*

Lin grimaced. "Well, I asked him. He was, um … he was quite upset, you know. I think maybe we were one of his last clients—maybe his only client—and he took it all very hard. But he did say he would *try* to come in, and yes to your next question: he maintains all the sales receipts, invoices, canceled checks—whatever—back in the cabinets in his and Juanita's office. There aren't any locks on the drawers, so you shouldn't have any trouble getting the folders."

"That's it?"

"Oh, to be clear, that's all the files we have readily available and covering the current year. See? I've asked one of the boys to bring down the prior year's files from upstairs because I didn't know if you'd need them today ... and Juanita's been after me to shred them anyway. See, that's them over there." Lin pointed toward the far corner where the elevator door stood propped open. One of the clerks was busy wheeling out tall stacks of cardboard storage boxes. "He's going to leave them outside the offices."

"You have only last year's records?"

"Yes, that's all Juanita said we needed right now. Is that OK?" The old man was looking stressed again.

"Well, I guess as long as the IRS never audits you ... I normally ask my clients to keep records for three years plus one. Four years, Lin. That's just being safe." Max shook his head and sighed. "Now let me go get Donna, and we'll get started."

• • •

Fifteen minutes later, Donna tapped at the upper glass half of the door. "Max, I need to talk with you," she demanded, scowling.

After he'd stepped down from the elevated office and they were well away from the salespeople and clerks, she continued, "What the hell am I supposed to be doing back there?"

Max looked about, making sure that no one else was near; she had whispered, but it was not a quiet whisper. *She's hissing at me.* He drew back. "Donna, I showed you the cash-register tape and how it's normally reconciled—what each line meant. Then I asked you to go back to Leonard's office and, until he arrives, leaf through the files looking for the daily reconciliation pages. I said there should be at least one page for each day, with the tape attached and the deposit slip attached to that. That's the way Leonard does it—or the way he once did it. At any rate, I want you to see what's available in the file cabinets, and when he arrives, we'll go over the last couple of days' cash postings to the cash-receipts journal—that's to show you how it's been done. You can change things later when you understand how it works."

Donna was direct. "There's not shit back there," she snarled.

"What?" He'd ceased whispering, too. "Show me!"

• • •

Fifteen more minutes passed, and Max was again in the elevated glass office, seated at the messy desk. Lin was sitting across from him, and Donna stood leaning against the doorframe, her arms crossed across her magnificent breasts. She was smirking.

"Lin, I'll tell you what we've found," he said. "There's virtually nothing concerning money—deposit slips, bank statements, not even petty-cash vouchers—in Juanita's desk drawers or in those boxes. In Leonard Green's office, we found purchase invoices, paid invoices, the same stuff you've got spread all over this desk, but virtually nothing concerning sales or cash receipts. I called Mr. Green at his house, explained where I was—I don't think he had any intention of coming here today, Lin—and asked about the documents in his files. You know what he said? 'Oh dear' is what he said. Just that: 'Oh dear.'"

Lin nervously patted his knee as he stared at the desktop. "I told you he was upset, didn't I?"

Max nodded. "Yes, yes, you did. But I'm not sure ... I think he's different—talking slower and more measured—from when I met with him before, back when I interviewed him for my classroom project ... and since. Do you think maybe he's had a stroke or something? Or maybe he knows something's gone wrong here—where's Juanita anyway? Shouldn't she be back from lunch already?"

Lin pushed himself up using the chair's arms for support. "I'll call," he simply replied. The old man seemed to have aged ten years ... in ten minutes. There was no longer a spring in his step or quickness to his movements. Even his blue, blue eyes appeared to have faded to the shade of a late-evening sky. "I'll call," he repeated.

The accountants watched as Lin punched in Juanita's home phone number from memory, standing there beside his beloved computer, using the phone on that table and turning his back to both Max and Donna. He didn't want them watching his face.

The phone rang … and rang. No one picked up. Lin turned back. "Doesn't seem to be anyone at home," he said, sounding bone-tired. "I've got a key. I'll send one of the fellows over." He looked to Max for affirmation. "Do you have time to stick around?"

Max said he did, but his associate said she didn't. "This is a pile of shit," Donna readily opined. "I've wasted all afternoon, I haven't eaten, and Nolan Smith will be very, very disappointed with this crap … Max." She could hardly wait to tell Nolan how his business partner had screwed up. *If this client was to be so important to our future, then we don't have a future. At least we don't have a combined future.* She'd say, "I bet Cooper's Electronics is bankrupt. I bet that old lady's robbed them blind and they can't even pay for our travel out there today! I bet Juanita cleaned out the bank and is long gone by now. I tried to tell you, Nolan. I tried to tell you! Some partner you chose."

Max pushed himself to his feet. "You can tell him whatever you think, Donna," he said quietly, guessing her thoughts. "I'm taking you back to the office and you can tell Nolan whatever comes to your little mind." He turned to Lin. "Please excuse us, sir. We'll—I'll be back as soon as possible."

● ● ●

While Max drove back to the electronics store, slowly negotiating the heavy late-afternoon Saint Pete traffic, Donna had taken a position on the front corner of Nolan Smith's desk while she shared the unfortunate events of the day, swinging her shapely legs to and fro as she talked and leaning far forward for maximum cleavage exposure. She was thoroughly enjoying her boss's seemingly rapt attention—even though he *had* pushed his chair far back against his credenza.

But contrary to her supposition, he was not really hearing her diatribe; he was actually engrossed in thoughts of his own, about his wife—she happened to be on her way in just then, driving to the office. She and Nolan had planned an early evening together: dinner and a movie—a real date. They'd talked earlier, and Valarie had understood the strains and stresses her husband was facing, that he definitely needed an evening's break. She knew he was having to make personnel changes in the office and had finally decided to dismiss a longtime employee, one who'd worked for him for over four years now. "That's surely a tough decision for any employer to make at any time," she'd said. "Maybe you can do it first thing tomorrow morning … and relax tonight."

●   ●   ●

At Cooper's Electronics, the clerk who'd earlier been dispatched to Juanita Jones's condo talked of his findings with Max, Lin, and Nathan in the elevated, half-glass office: "No one answered the door, see, so I called the cops—she could have fallen or something. And we got the complex's custodian to open her door because the key you gave me didn't fit. Well, sir, there was no one in there, and the drawers in the bedroom were all pulled out. It looked to me like she'd left real quick, real quick, and that was what the cops thought, too. There were a couple of small suitcases on the bed in the big bedroom—but clothes and such? Those were all gone. Books, too. There were some books left behind, though, pulled out of shelves and thrown all around the place. Nothing personal. Just, like, library books and paperbacks. Novels. Nothing personal. In fact, the cops said there didn't appear to be any personal stuff at all in the place. Except for this here letter … care of you, Mr. Cooper." He held out the envelope.

Lin took it, reading his name written in large cursive letters behind the "c/o" marking on the front. "That'd be me all right. Didn't the police want to see what's inside? What was written?"

"They'd left already," the clerk said.

"You want to open it, Lin?"

The old man, now looking like he hadn't slept in days, slowly shook his head. "No, it's addressed to you, Max, on the next line. See there? Besides, there might be some smallpox powder in there." He chuckled wearily as the accountant sat bolt upright in his chair. "No, no, just kidding. Anyway, I imagine Juanita doesn't have anything more to say to me ... or about me. *You* could read it aloud, you know."

Max nodded. "I will." He took the letter, placed it flat on the desk, and slowly slid the blade of his pocketknife down the top of the flap. Then he held his breath and tapped the envelope several times on the desk's surface (*just in case*) before removing and unfolding the enclosed stationery.

"'I'll kill you, you son of a bitch,'" he slowly read, his voice flat. He flipped the letter over to check the reverse side. "That's it. That's all she wrote. Now, that is really disturbing."

"Frightens you?" Nathan asked.

"No, she misspelled *bitch*. Forgot the *t*. See there?" He held up the stationery for the other men's perusals.

"Yeah," Lin agreed. "Imagine how she's messed up my books if she can't even spell."

• • •

A month later, Lin, Nathan, and Max again gathered in the high office; Nolan had joined them for this meeting.

"Based on the current period's revenues and collections," Max said, "we've estimated that Juanita has skimmed approximately one hundred thousand dollars ... per year. Considering that she's worked for Cooper's Electronics for over twenty years," he said, nodding toward Lin, "well, you can multiply for yourself. So … I'd say you've got a business that's much more profitable than you thought."

"That's not after taxes," Lin dryly noted.

• • •

Another month passed, and Nolan handed his partner an unsigned letter; it had come in the office mail and was addressed to Max's attention.

"'I'll kill you, you son of a bitch,'" he read aloud. He tilted back in his chair and looked up. "Suppose this one's from Donna Goldner, Mr. Smith?"

"Suppose so, Mr. Anderson. I don't think *she* has a problem with the spelling of that word."

CHAPTER 7
EVENING

'm standing beside her desk. "Please, Allison," I whine. "Please don't start reading another chapter right now. You've finished the 1983 one, and I've still got to drive back out to Gulfport before it gets too late. I want to walk around the house again before it's too dark."

"It's your own fault, Cole," she replies without looking up. "You told me to read this chapter next; it's not my fault it's a long one. So don't blame me for taking up your afternoon.

"By the way," she continues, her voice going higher at the end (her teasing tone), "do you have an idea where this Nathan Dawson might live today?" She's leafing back through the manuscript pages as if she's hunting for the reference.

I laugh. "You think you could be interested in an older feller now? You know he's got to be … about my age. And wasn't that you telling me that you'd become something of a … what do they call it now? A cougar? Is that the right predator?"

She gazes up at me. Seconds pass slowly as she holds my eye and considers her responses. She allows her chair to swing fully upright—she'd been reading with her shoes off and her feet resting in the bottom drawer.

"Well, you know, I was just wondering," she replies, now smiling sweetly and shrugging—her coquettish pose. It's one of my favorites. But it doesn't seem to quite fit with the earlier expression—the reflective one. She's leaving thoughts unsaid. I wonder why.

Anyway, I chuckle and grin in return. "I guess I could introduce you two—"

Allison straightens. "Is he real? I mean, do you think he's an actual person around here?" She's really surprised. "I mean, I thought most of those stories," she says, waggling a finger toward the bulging file that now rests on her desk, "were, you know, fictional. Mostly imagination. I didn't know if certain characters were, you know, made up—for color."

I'm still grinning. "Well, maybe they are … or maybe they mostly are. However, relating to that story you've just finished reading, I happen to know of a stereo-equipment business located but a few blocks from here, with an exterior very similar to that described in the chapter." I nod at the stapled pages in her hands. "And, in fact, a few years ago I happened to visit said edifice in search of a replacement part for my aging McIntosh amplifier … inside that very store … and was assisted by a salesperson with an appearance much like that of Mr. Dawson in the story. And, in fact, in a more recent time and again in need of—"

"Cole!" Allison's losing patience.

"—a stereo component, I went there and met the owner of the establishment. Remember him?" I nod meaningfully at the pages in her hands. I can't remember the guy's name at the moment, but she should know whom I mean. "The other elderly chap in the story?"

"So, the salesman … he's Nathan Dawson? In the story?"

"Tall, distinguished, wearing a three-piece suit—yeah, I'd say that's him. And elderly. Did I mention he's an elderly dude?"

Allison folds her hands and snickers. "Why, I believe one Lieutenant Eltie may be … a little bit jealous?" She glances up.

"Am not," I reply. A childish retort for sure, but that's all I can think to say. I resist the urge to repeat the words.

"Yes. Yes, I think you are. You're—" The phone rings, and she automatically snatches up the handset. "—jealous. And I think that's sooo cute. That and the fact that you can't remember Lin Cooper's name." She pulls a silly face and taps her temple with her forefinger before pushing the blinking line button.

"Lieutenant Bryce," she announces into the mouthpiece, her tone now completely businesslike, neutral. "Yes?" she continues in another tone—a softer voice. "Who's calling? Oh, hello, Mike. Yes. Yes. Forensics—of course I remember you."

So much for business, I think. *Great timing, too.*

She flutters her eyelashes at me and grins wickedly—like the Cheshire cat—with a smile full of teeth. She's letting me know that Caller Mike is the guy from downstairs who so admired her legs. "Yes, yes, go ahead. I'm ready," she says. She slips a pad of paper from her top drawer and, for the next full minute, scribbles madly on its lined pages. "Of course. Of course. And thank you. What? Well … we'll have to see, won't we?" She giggles like a schoolgirl and daintily returns the handset to its cradle. "Hummmm …"

I scowl down at her.

"What?" She pretends to have just now noticed the expression on my face.

"Nothing," I answer, with a tad more force than I intend.

"'And you've picked up a bit of an attitude, still curious and willing to learn, I hope,'" she purrs.

"My gosh, you quote the Cheshire cat, too?" It's my turn to be surprised.

"I rented the movie after the last time you commented on my smile. Bought the book, too."

That sets me to guffawing along with her. All this time, I didn't think she was half listening to me.

"And now," she announces, while I'm still whewing and wiping my eyes, "it's time to get back to it. Time to do what we're getting paid for. Like I said, time now for you to learn." She swings about to face her desk and begins pushing together the sheets and packets that litter its surface, straightening the grouped pages and returning them to the folder. "Forensics said they were not able to tie the prints on that gun," she says, waving two fingers over her shoulder toward the picture of the Beretta on my desk, "to any prints on file ... only to the decedent's prints." She'd paused for effect, giving me time to digest the information. "They're saying the dead guy was holding the gun at some point in time," she explains.

Another lengthy pause.

"Yes? I heard you; I understand. What else?"

"So then maybe, when the guy was shot in the face, he reflexively jerked back, throwing the pistol onto the porch roof where they discovered it." She mimics the movement without turning.

I sit against the edge of her desk and puff my cheeks in thought. "Yeah. Yeah ... I can see that happening ... from the way he was facing and all. Allison, I'd say your conjecture is logical and valid." We nod in unison.

"And the prints on the gas can?" I ask. "Did good ol' Forensics Mike have anything to say about them?"

"Yes. Also matches the decedent's prints. At some points in time, the dead guy held both the Beretta and the gasoline container."

I mentally sort through the characters in Max's book-to-be. "So then a large male, the decedent, comes to the house, into the yard, holding a gun and a can filled with gasoline. And holding religious pamphlets. Happens all the time, wouldn't you say?" I resist adding, "Convert or die, heathen!" with my fist raised high overhead; sarcasm is best when it's subtle. Besides, at the moment, Allison appears distant, deep in her own thoughts: her desk is clear, her eyes are closed ... and she's stroking her chin—as I tend to do when I'm thinking—except she doesn't have two days of beard stubble on her chin to stroke. I wait for her to answer.

"Well, I suppose that does explain why the dead guy had the Jehovah's Witness material," she softly allows, having totally ignored my witticism. "He needed something ... to get him inside the house. It was daylight, wasn't it." Her question is actually a statement.

"Yes. Daytime," I confirm anyway.

"You know what I think?" she blurts, refocusing on me, her ruminations now complete. "I think the dead man is ... Gordon Moore! Yes! Mr. ... Gordon ... Moore."

"What?" I'm astonished and doubtful. "Gordon Moore? That guy from the story, from, eh, Randal Minz's office? Other than his being an obese person, how would you ...? Say, did good ol' Forensics Mike have more to say on the phone?" I'm trying to see her pad; she's a fantastic detective but—

She grins furiously, and her eyes flick upward: she's mocking me. Apparently ol' Allison has not fully returned to her business mode, the dark side. "See," she explains, "that's Forensics' take on the situation—their speculations and thoughts. Mike just relayed the info to me on the phone." She turns her notepad in my direction. "He said they'd had some success with tracing the serial number on the gun. There had been just enough of the number left to make it out."

I remember seeing the scratches where someone had tried to file away the gun's identifying number. I stand and reach over for my glossy print and lift it to the light.

"And?" I ask. It's my turn to hasten the story.

"Recall reading about Gordon Moore?" she asks, patting the thick sheaf of papers.

"Yeah, yeah. He's in that first story you read this morning: an accountant who once worked with Max ... on his first job." A memory strobe flashes in my brain. "He was fired because of Max, wasn't he? I mean, in the story. He deserved it, but ... was that his real name?" It's my turn to ask the question.

"Guess so. Maybe Max Anderson, the author, hasn't yet bothered to change *any* of the names in these typed pages. Or maybe he's kept the names to remind him of the personalities of the people he knew, and maybe he's only changed them in the proof copies that went to the publisher. You did say the original is in the publisher's hands, didn't you?"

I nod. "Yeah. Yeah. They're sending us proof copies."

"So his name really is Nathan Dawson," Allison moons.

"The elderly Nathan Dawson," I interject. "But as you said, 'Now's the time to get to it'—or something like that. We now need to make haste and procure a court order to search Mr. Moore's abode and—"

She's shaking her head. "Not necessary right now if you want to revisit the scene first," she says. "Mike said Forensics has already made a positive match: the dead guy *is* Mr. Moore. See, in addition to the gun's registration, it seems Gordon has—had—records on file with the hospital, and, with those records, they've made an affirmative DNA comparison. I guess he's given blood and signed releases and so on—the hospital could share the records with us."

"And the names matched," I repeat. "So you weren't really conjecturing, were you? You weren't connecting the proverbial dots."

She smiles and shakes her head, still obviously quite pleased with herself. She'd had me going all right; she had the better joke. She had me believing she could return from vacation and, within a few hours on the first day, solve my—*hey! Wait!*

"Allison?" I ask. "Does good ol' Mike know who shot good ol' Gordon Moore dead in the front yard? Have they located any nine-millimeter bullet holes in tree trunks or fences, because *that* gun *was* recently discharged, too?"

"Cole, did you—"

"Yeah, I sniffed it before they bagged it for evidence," I confess. "But I didn't screw up anything." She knows me too well. At times, I've been known to borrow from the evidence locker for additional, after-hours examinations. Impulsive and impatient according to her. Thinking outside the box according to me. "See, Allison, that's why we need to go back to the house now. We missed finding the shell casings and the slugs. Now that we know that Mr. Moore was carrying this pistol, I'm betting he went down firing at his killer." I show the photo. "Now, if that happened to have been Mr. Anderson using his shotgun for more than snakes—"

"His neighbor shot the king snake," Allison interrupts. "And that's his neighbor's shotgun."

"OK. If that was Mr. Anderson using his neighbor's shotgun," I continue, staring hard at her, "to shoot an intruder, who'd surprised him by trying to break through the *back* door of his house—"

"Why do you think Gordon first tried to come in the back door?" she interrupts again.

I take a heavy breath; this debate is exhausting. "The blood droplets and footprints around the house. And the mass of pellet holes in the siding beside the back windows, you know, as if Gordon had spotted Anderson through the window in the back bedroom and took a shot ... never mind."

"Gordon had the pistol," she helpfully corrects.

"That's why I said never mind," I growl. (I've never quite mastered the rueful-response technique.) "Maybe ... never mind. I'll have to think more on that. Maybe the neighbor—"

"He shot the birdhouse from the other direction. You know, you're determined to make the pellets in the siding a principal part of this story."

I shake my head. "Forget the pellets. I'll have to think more on that. Anyway," I continue with my speculation, "say ol' Gordon surprises Max at the back of the house ... and Gordon also has a shotgun! Max runs out the front door and runs smack into Gordon coming around the side of the house from the back. He takes away Gordon's shotgun. Bang! Bang! It's all over. Max one and Gordon zero."

Allison gives me her scrunched-eye look; she's clearly not persuaded. She pulls open her desk drawer to retrieve her purse and stands. "Come on," she orders. "Let's get to Gulfport before it's too dark to see. Maybe we'll find a bullet hole at the front of the house—one that Forensics missed. But I'm not buying your analysis because there are just too many holes—pardon the pun. Direction. Like you said, dead Gordon was facing the wrong direction if he launched the pistol onto the roof. See, if Max had burst through the front door and blasted him in the face, he'd have been facing the other direction, and the gun would have been in the street. And, besides, something has happened to Mr. Anderson. Yes, he's an accountant and probably runs from his own shadow, but I just cannot see him as having panicked and then taken off for the hills. Remember the tow-truck police report? No, Cole, I think you were more correct before, when you thought there was another person involved, maybe an accomplice. I don't see fat Gordon, an accountant who's so brave that he keys cars in the dead of night for revenge, as having the balls to commit murder by himself."

I involuntarily wince with her harsh reference to the male anatomy. I mean I'm not a prude, and I've heard worse—particularly from her—but maybe I see the reference as being unnecessary in communicating her idea—unnecessary verbiage. *My gosh! I'm becoming Allison!* I smile with the thought.

Allison glares at me. She's watching my face, notes my slight distress, and, as usual, has guessed at my thoughts. But she's guessed wrong this time if she thinks I'm offended. Because I'm not.

"Come on, asshole!" she abruptly commands.

She also says I put women on pedestals and I should know better. She says it pisses her off when I do it, so she's toughening me—she thinks. Maybe she's mostly right. Or maybe we were simply brought up on opposite sides of the Mason-Dixon Line, and I'm simply too old to "toughen." It can happen, you know. I once told Allison that, somewhere along the way, she'd missed out on the grasping of certain admirable human concepts, such as empathy or sympathy. She said she didn't care either way, God bless the woman.

• • •

The drive to Anderson's house is quick. Rush hour is over, and traffic flows freely in our direction. I speak my thoughts aloud some more with Allison as we drive along, about how the can of gasoline is actually a better fit with Gordon's MO of indirect aggression: his avoidance of direct contact with his victims. He'd most certainly planned to set Max's house on fire once he determined the man to be inside—or maybe it hadn't matter at all to him if Max *was not* inside? Like if the vengeful idea of keying another man's car was destruction of his property, so would be the burning of his house.

"An understatement," Allison notes. "And the pistol?"

"Only an emergency escape option," I confidently reply. "He could have justified that scenario to himself."

Allison says she will stick with her accomplice theory.

We pull in close to the granite curbing along the front of the Gulfport lot; our unmarked car is facing the wrong direction on the avenue. No matter: cops don't write tickets around here for parking on the opposite side of the street.

I get out, and Allison meets me at the front of the car—she's also not a woman who'd deign to await the gentlemanly opening of her car door. I'd tried it once.

We cross the narrow strip of lawn to the sidewalk and the still-open gate; no one had yet felt the need to secure the fence. Or to sweep up the glass from the road; it crunched beneath the soles of our shoes. I lift the yellow crime-scene tape, and we enter the yard; I close the gate behind.

"How much longer do you think they'll keep the tape up?" I absently ask.

"Probably until we tell Forensics to take it down," Allison opines. "Or until someone asks. This is actually my first front-yard murder, so I really don't know."

We stop at the outline of the murder victim spray-painted onto the sidewalk and grass.

"Yeah, you're right," I say, acknowledging her earlier conclusion. "Gordon was angled such that the blast must have come from the road." I turn and look in that direction, at the glass shards glistening in the fading light. I look back to her.

She shrugs. "Maybe the accomplice shot him?"

There are no answers that seem to make sense. And what has happened to Anderson?

• • •

A half hour passes, and we've slowly circled the house at least five times, pausing only to probe at nail holes in the wood trim or to brush at dark spots in the grass. I've also collected additional bloodstain samples from the walkway by the side of the house in anticipation of another Forensics screwup. I can easily imagine ol' Mike adulterating another sampling of key evidential material, such is the distraction of his fiery loins.

"A sixth time?" Allison asks. She knows me.

"Yeah."

I cross my arms and rock from side to side, thinking. "Yeah," I say again, "and then we'll go home. We've about done all we can, and if we take a quick gander in the garage—who's that?" I see a dark shape tromping toward us, rounding the corner of the house, maybe coming from the alley. The man freezes when he sees me.

"Hello, sir!" I call out, lightly waving to him with my free hand.

"Ohhhh shit!" he yelps in reply. He turns, scurrying toward the shadows of the garage. Allison catches up to him before he's even halfway across the yard.

As I limp closely behind, I can see that he's an older man—a fellow I immediately recognize when he turns.

"Well, hello there," I gasp, when I finally make it within earshot of the pair; Allison's holding the old guy's elbow with one hand and her badge with the other. "Fancy seeing you again ... Mr. Max Anderson."

I remember him from years before, when I was a rookie cop assigned to investigate leads involving organized criminal activities in the Tampa Bay area. I remember his startled face: I had seen it once before when I'd been dispatched to a warehouse on the south side of Saint Petersburg—an alleged importing monopoly that had turned out to be nothing more than a Mickey Mouse, single-man bottling operation.

So now I know why Max's olive-oil story had seemed so oddly familiar to me when I'd read it. And he had seen me years before, too, and had written of me from his perspective, having then mistaken me for one of Trafficanti's soldiers: I'm one of his characters in those chapters, his book! Imagine that.

And I remember having seen Max Anderson a year later, too: I'd been assigned to huddle with some crackpot who'd claimed he had inside info on the mafia operations in Tampa—Trafficanti's mob again. I'd met up with the dude at a Jewish funeral on the north side of Saint Pete—and the guy had turned out to be as big a loony as I'd expected. I don't remember the informant's name ... but I remember Max.

And he remembers me, too, because I've obviously alarmed him, causing him to shuffle off like that. And I was so much bigger back then, when I lifted weights and all. *Funny.* "Hah!" I snort aloud.

And I'm staring at that same scared-shitless face again.

"So what's so humorous?" Allison asks. "And how do you know—"

I ignore her. "Sorry, Mr. Anderson. No need for alarm. We all just need to sit down together ... and talk. Umm, got any tea and cookies inside?"

"Eh, yeah, OK," he manages to mumble.

• • •

Another half hour has passed, and we're still sitting around Max's kitchen table. We've explained to him why his property is encircled with all the pretty yellow crime-scene tape and have, in turn, received very few answers to our many questions. In short, he's clueless as to any of the recent events inside that tape.

"See, after I finished my book," he explains, "I decided I needed to take some time off to visit a buddy up in Yankeetown and—didn't my daughter say anything about where I was? I told her where I was going and that I'd be away for a couple of days. I'd still be there fishing, but when the old man at the camp store asked me if I had a brother who'd recently been murdered, well, I thought I'd better come back early. As usual, I couldn't reach my daughter to get more information about it—the news story on the radio." He shakes his head.

"A day or so ago, remember when you were packing for your trip?" I ask. "Did you hear or see any activity out your back bedroom window? A loud noise like a gunshot perhaps? Or maybe a car backfire?"

Max smiles gently. "Well, sir, I'm a bit deaf in my left ... no, I'm deaf as a bat. No, wait. That wouldn't be deaf at all, would it? Let's just say, when my battery goes," he points to his ear, "I can't hear thunder. So, if you were banging on my bedroom door with a baseball bat, I just might hear you ... but I might not, too."

"Did you bolt and lock your doors before you left to go to Yankeetown?" Allison asks, between scribbles on the lined pad. She takes a quick sip from her mug—her third cup of tea.

If I drank tea like that at this hour of the evening, I might as well take a pillow and go sleep in the bathroom. That is, if I could go to sleep at all. I lift the teapot and refill her cup.

"Thanks, Cole. Good tea, Mr. Anderson."

"You're welcome, ma'am. But just Max, please," he corrects, giving her his best endearing smile. "Just Max. And I'm glad you like the tea. I can't drink much of it, or I might as well sleep in the bathtub. I definitely envy you your bladder.

"Now, about locking my doors. I believe my front door was already locked. See, when I was leaving the house, a big fellow was knocking at it; I could see him and his fistful of pamphlets through the front window—he'd just turned to go. He musta been selling stuff or wanting to talk religion—we get a lot of 'em around here. But with my hearing-aid battery dead, there wasn't any use of me running after him and inviting him in since I couldn't hear him anyway. So, I just slipped out the back way to the garage."

"Did you see anybody out back?" I ask. I'm still betting that someone had tried to plug him through the bedroom window. Allison guesses my thought and sighs deeply, looking to the ceiling.

"Well, actually, yeah," he says. "There was a lady in a car blocking my garage door—but she left about the same time I raised it. Tore off down the alley, she did, and about ran over the neighbor's garbage can. She wanted to get someplace quick, I guess. Took a hard left onto the street and another left—like she was going in the wrong direction and wanted to circle the block out front. I kinda watched after her."

"Think of anything else?" Allison asks. "Anyone else coming around? Anything strange?"

"Well, yeah. I wasn't going to say anything, but I think the old fellow next door has poured kerosene or something alongside my house. I noticed, when I came in tonight, that my flowers are all dead along that corner and the grass is all brown like something was poured along the wall there. See, I had to get after him the other day—right before I left—for carting a leaky can of red paint around the side there to my garage. He wanted to give the paint to me—thought I could use it. See, he's a nice old guy, but he needs someone to look in on him periodically." Max's expression turns hopeful. "Say, anything you folks can do? I mean I don't want him to hurt himself, and I'm afraid if he's got combustibles lying about, he just might catch himself on fire. Understand?"

Allison smiles. "I'll ask and get back to you. OK?" She leans my way and whispers, "There's your blood on the pavers. Maybe you should get those samples back from Forensics before they test 'em?" Her smile broadens.

I finger the additional samples in the evidence bags in my coat pocket as I look about the room, searching for a trash can.

"Hey, Lieutenant Eltie, you should show Max the scar on your hand," she suggests, now no longer whispering. "You know, the one you got from a shotgun's slide mechanism."

"I got an old shotgun over there," Max replies, pointing to the hallway. "It's my neighbor's. Want it, you say?"

Thank God he can hardly hear.

"No," I say. "The lady's trying to be humorous for us."

"Oh? Beauty and personality, too? That's nice. Back in my day, the police officers were not near as attractive as this lovely lady." The old lech sends another toothy smile Allison's way.

She's grinning back! And patting his mottled old arm! "Sir?" I say, nudging his other arm, trying to get him back on subject. "Max?"

He turns back to me—reluctantly. "Yes, Lieutenant Eltie?"

"Perhaps you can tell me more about the woman in the car?" I venture. "The one who was blocking your garage door when you were leaving? What'd she look like? And the car—do you remember anything about the vehicle? Tinted windows rolled up? Color? Anything?" It's too much to hope that the old guy noticed the license plate. And even more to think he would remember it.

Max drops his watery eyes to the tabletop and fidgets with his teacup for a minute. He's giving his memory a workout for sure. He looks up and focuses in on my face.

"Well, sir," he begins, "when you're my age, you tend to dis-remember car models after 1970; they look too much alike these days. But the lady's car, I'd say, was a late-model Ford Taurus SHO. A 2014 or maybe a 2015. Rental, I expect: it looked too clean and plain. You know, since they stopped using distinctive county numbers in the Florida automobile tags, it's kind of hard to spot cars coming from the airport rental these days. Anyway, that was just my observation. And she'd tried to put a cloth or paper over the plate anyway—to hide the numbers, I guess. That's why I watched her when she tore out—that and her almost takin' out my neighbor's can. Color? Silver. Tinted windows? Not very much. Rolled up, too." He looks again to the table and watches himself stir his tea.

"You know," he continues, "there *was* something about that lady. She was staring so hard at the back of the house, concentrating on it so hard, that she looked right past me, past the garage. And there was something familiar about her … maybe I'll remember in a while. Oh! There was one other thing: you said something about a car backfire? Yeah, when I was closing my bedroom window, I maybe heard a backfire. Bang! About the same time I turned the handle there. Bang! Startled me; I thought my window had broken or something, but it hadn't. Then, when I saw the big guy at the front, I thought it had been him beating on the front door. But, you know, that'd have to have been pretty close—and loud—for me to have heard it. Do you suppose *that* was actually a gunshot?"

"Could have been," I say.

"Been a while since I'd heard something like that." Max is back to stirring his tea, watching it swirl in the cup. "You know, the neighborhood's actually calmed down a bit over the years." He looks up. "My back gate's been left open, too. I saw it tonight when I drove in. Of course it could have been Mr. Adams, my neighbor. That's why I thought maybe he'd splashed something along the front of my house."

• • •

More time passes, and Allison and I are on our way back to the station. She'd called Forensics and received their permission to allow Mr. Anderson to reoccupy his house tonight. Good thing. It's dark now, and the old guy would've had a tough time finding a motel room this late in the evening. And I told him I'd swing back by tomorrow to roll up the yellow tape for him.

"Took that situation pretty well, wouldn't you say?" Allison says, talking over the road noise.

"Old Max? Yeah, I'd say so. But, then again, I really didn't expect him to be too rattled. He's had some pretty rugged life experiences, if his stories are any indication. Rugged for an accountant, that is." I remember his toothy grin.

"Yeah? So which story should I read next?"

"You *do* know we still have a murderer to catch, don't you?"

"Just for background, Cole. Which chapters should I read for more background?"

"You *do* know he's writing to make himself appear in the most favorable light, don't you? And we really don't know the extent of factual content in those stories. Veracity," I add.

"I'm familiar with the term, Lieutenant Eltie. So then don't make a recommendation; I'll pick my own."

I sniff. "Try the boatbuilder then. The one who smuggles in bales of pot. I thought that one was mostly believable. Or the pill mill slash record shop—that one's probably even more realistic. The preacher's wife and tax fraud? That one was boring. Oh yeah! Try the one where his client takes him to the strip club in Miami—that was a good one." I glance over at Allison. Maybe I was a bit too enthusiastic with that last referral?

Then her phone rings, and she answers, "Lieutenant Bryce. Yes, Mike. Yes. Yes. We're on our way back to the station now. Silver? What? Say again!" She's got her pad out now and is scribbling hard. She clicks on the visor light. "Yes. Got it. Yes, we'll walk down as soon as we get there." She closes her phone and returns to her notes.

"Got a date with ol' Mikey?" I coolly ask. She hadn't sounded overly familiar on this phone conversation … and I didn't want to start something. I wait as she finishes her scratching.

"OK. We've got a lead, Cole. Or perhaps the solution to this case."

She's ignoring my question. Figures.

"What? So tell me," I order. I sense she's about to make this a learning experience for me, too. And we're still several miles from the station.

"We're both correct," she begins, "partially. You believe the murderer might have first happened onto Mr. Anderson from the backyard, seeing him through the bedroom window as he was inside packing for his trip to Yankeetown." She angles her pad in the weak light, trying to read her own writing, and makes a correction to a word. "There. So the murderer, having entered through the rear gate—remember Max said Mr. Adams may have left it open?—and having scouted around the exterior of the house, sees Mr. Anderson through the window and hurriedly fires a shotgun blast at the target now exiting the bedroom—a single shotgun blast at a distance.

Maybe Mr. Anderson *had* heard someone knocking at his door, and perhaps that visitor saved his life."

"Oops, oops," I grunt. I brake for the red light with more-than-normal force; I'd been listening to Allison and almost missed the changing of the signal at the intersection. "Sorry 'bout that. Go on," I urge. "So the murderer's stomping around the yard would explain the footprints I noticed at the side of the house. The open gate. The chewed-up wood at the side of the window. Was it birdshot?"

"Buckshot," she immediately replies; she doesn't have to refer to her notes for that information. "Buckshot—just like you said." Allison's being charitable.

"Maybe it's Gordon Moore's accomplice?" I say. I can be charitable, too.

"No, no, I don't think so." Allison's referring to her notes again. "I think the killer must have seen Max moving toward the front door and, having missed the target, raced around the house to intercept the to-be-departing victim."

"Ran around the house. Gotcha. And ran around to find Gordon blocking his way."

"Drove around … and *her* way."

The strobe flashes again in my brain. "The woman Max saw in the Taurus! She shot at him, missed, and ran to her car to catch him in the front. Yeah! And ol' Gordon was walking down the walkway toward the road, having been unable to draw Max to the front door. Wow! That'd be some coincidence."

"The woman in the vehicle screeches to a halt in the street," Allison continues for me, "alarming Gordon, who tosses away the metal can he'd been using to sprinkle gasoline along the front corner of the house—or he might have heard the gunshot in the rear. Anyway, he brandishes his pistol, which, in turn, alarms the woman in the car. She raises her shotgun and, as Gordon blasts out her side window and windshield, returns fire—a single shot using full choke. It catches him in the face. He jerks his arm upward, sending his side-arm to the porch roof … and he then assumes the supine position on the concrete walk." She soundlessly dusts her hands together, signaling the end.

"The glass in the street?"

"Car windows from a Ford product."

I hadn't seen Forensics taking glass samples. "And do we know the assailant lady's identity?" I chance. *Good ol' Mike's been busy.*

"It wasn't Mike I was talking to," she says, once more having delved into my thoughts. "That was his boss who called. See, this afternoon, we received an alert about a vehicle having departed the roadway on the Skyway. But no one had actually witnessed the accident. Rather, a fisherman, wading through the mangroves behind one of the picnic areas, spotted the car in the water—a silver automobile—and called it in. A twelve-gauge Remington shotgun was also found on the floorboard of the car."

"So that explains how you knew Gordon Moore had opened fire on the car and blown out its windows." I chuckle. "And that kind of made it easier for the woman to return fire at Gordon, too, I guess—or at the man she thought was Max."

"Strange how things work out sometimes, huh?"

"And the woman, Allison? What does she have against Mr. Anderson?"

"She was afraid Max's tell-all book was going to ruin her marriage. Her career. She had respectability, fame, fortune—you name it. She'd read the *Times* article ... and snapped, I guess. She'd flown into Clearwater from Tallahassee—her husband's a politician—and rented a car—"

"Wait!" I interrupt. "How'd she get a shotgun on an airplane? And what's her name?" I'm getting confused again. "Was the woman still in the car out by the Skyway?"

"Yeah," Allison allows. "She'd caught a nine-millimeter slug through the car door, and, apparently, in trying to return to the Saint Pete–Clearwater Airport, she made a wrong turn and ended up going south. So, she's losing blood and trying to turn around—she ran off the road and bled to death … out of sight behind the man-groves in about three feet of water."

"The woman's name?"

"Donna Farris."

"The governor's wife?"

"Yes. You'll remember her as Donna Goldner."

"Wow!" I rub my forehead as the car horn blares behind us. It continues to squall as its owner swings his vehicle into the adjacent lane to detour around us, giving me the middle finger as he passes. *Serves me right,* I think. I have no idea how many light cycles we've sat through.

"Wow!" I repeat as we lurch forward. "Wow! Donna Goldner. Well, she certainly hated Max … even before he wrote his book. And she certainly sounded a bit unhinged. But to want to kill him?"

"Yeah," Allison agrees. "Maybe I could have foreseen this if, say, it involved the political-party chairwoman—no, no, I couldn't. This is too extreme."

I snort in agreement. "Maybe you should read that chapter next. Now *that* woman and her minions could easily have—no, I shouldn't say any more; that would mess up the story for you."

"I will read it," she asserts. "Hey! There's the station—pull into the front parking area. They're waiting on us in the chief's office."

"Will the guys from Forensics be joining us?"

"Yes, they said they had a lead on … the other assailant, too."

"Other assailant?"

"Someone named Sherman-Williams. You know. That company that makes—"

"I know what they make!" *Crap! No need to retrieve those "blood" samples now.* Allison's facing away from me, staring at something out her window. Her shoulders are shaking. *Crap!*

• • •

www.ingramcontent.com/pod-product-compliance
Lightning Source LLC
Chambersburg PA
CBHW050943120626
46552CB00001B/357